E.D.F Chronicles - E.D.F Resurgent

Mankind had turned the tables on their brutal Krenaran invaders, although the outer colonies were reduced to little more than rubble. Humanity continued the fight-back aided by their Solarian allies, planet by planet, sector by sector the E.D.F were pushing back the tide. However the greatest battle had yet to be fought, Gamma IV, a strategically vital planet supplying vast amounts of arms and equipment to E.D.F troops and repairs to its naval vessels was in danger of falling into the hands of the enemy. If it fell, the loss of equipment and facilities could have a disastrous effect on the war effort. The E.D.F could not and would not let that happen, Michael Alexander and Nikolai Vargev had no idea of the scale of the battle that awaited them.

First published in Great Britain in 2011 by Lulu, this edition published 2012 by Invigilus press.

A copy of this book is available from the British library

ISBN# 978-0-9574705-1-4

By Ian J. Smethurst

E.D.F Chronicles : The Krenaran massacre
E.D.F Chronicles : E.D.F Resurgent.

E.D.F Chronicles - E.D.F Resurgent

Ian J. Smethurst

For Carol and Geoff,

For being a light in dark places.

Contents.

1. Michael's loss

Michael Alexander was sat at the bar of the 'black hole', a bar-cum-meeting place aboard Delta base. It was a reasonably large open plan area, and one of the more popular haunts on the station. Surprisingly, it escaped major damage from the utter devastation wrought on the massive installation by repeated Krenaran attacks just over eight months ago. Even now repairs were still ongoing in some of the more badly damaged sections of the station. It was finally adjudged by E.D.F command that it was sufficiently operational again to resume its role as fleet command installation for the navy barely three weeks ago.

Although right now the black hole was quiet, only a handful of other men talked and drank. In the background soft jazz music was playing, though Michael; not being particularly schooled in the jazz players, had no idea who played it. He had come here for one purpose, and one purpose alone; to forget.

Having just arrived back from an escort mission with a small flotilla of converted Lincoln class supply ships carrying a force of E.D.F troops from the 8th 'black jacks' infantry company to the fighting around the Aurelias colony. It had been a fairly routine mission, with only a little resistance around Aurelias itself.

He was nursing a scotch; rolling the small whisky tumbler around with his fingers and contemplating the past. Of happier times, before he had become haunted by the loss of his wife Jana, and his son Theo.

Most nights when he slept, he would dream that he was still with them; tonight would be no different. Some nights would be worse; asleep, he would long for them to come back, seeing their faces in his dreams. Then he would awake, and know they couldn't for they were now dead; it didn't make it any easier, the sense of loss was devastating.

He had celebrated his 35th birthday last week; alone, nursing a scotch just as he did tonight.

"Would ya' mind if I pulled up a chair next to ya' cap'n?" said a familiar Irish sounding voice. It was Lieutenant Commander Quinn Kinraid.

Michael silently gestured for the tall, ginger haired man to have a seat.

Quinn had been hand picked to be second officer on board the Liberty, after Televis had been placed in command of the Solarian battle cruiser Faeriath. He was a tall man at 6 feet 5 inches, and had a long mane of flowing auburn curls which ran just past his shoulders, held together in a tight ponytail, he also sported a medium length yet neatly trimmed goatee. Personally chosen by Michael; they had been long time friends, but also Kinraid was a hell of an officer and could more than handle the ship when Michael wasn't around.

"Ya' lookin' kind a down to me sir, if ya' beg ma' pardon."

"I miss them Quinn........I miss them a lot."

"'Tis the tragedy of war so it is; not all wounds can be healed, sir."

"Ten months on and I still miss them. I remember them like they were still here."

Michael and Quinn had already talked about the deaths of Jana and Theo, although Quinn had barely been serving on the Liberty a little over a month. The commander had explained that at an early age, he had lost his mother in a chemical leak at a local research laboratory in Aberdeen, and had spent the rest of his life before the E.D.F, with his father in Dublin.

Michael drained what remained of the whisky, and stared blankly at the empty glass, it reminded him of his empty life.

The viewer blazed into action, directly across from where the two were sitting, the brightness of the screen cast an almost eerie glow across the bar, as well as the two men's faces.

"This is the outer colony news service, I am Annika Raumov; the headlines today. The war continues to go well for the E.D.F - Solarian alliance, and notable victories at the Perseus and Malthus colonies have been recorded. We take you now to General Macken of the 14th E.D.F battalion 'head hunters' to describe the engagements."

The picture changed to a young looking man, barely in his thirties, his camouflaged features stained with the soot and grime of battle.

"Generals are getting younger everyday," Michael pointed out, before turning his attention back to the viewer.

"Thank you. The Malthus victory was a textbook rapid deployment. Firstly E.D.F and Solarian naval forces drove the Krenaran ships back, and quickly launched God-hammer bomber squadrons to knock out any Krenaran air defences on the surface. Once this was complete Stockholm class landers deployed almost seven hundred troops and one hundred armoured vehicles to the surface, to commence the ground war in conjunction with God-hammer bomber raids; the colony was re-captured within three days."

"So they finally re-took Malthus," Michael raised an eyebrow, "funny how they don't tell you the casualties."

"Or what ships we mighta' lost buying their way in."

"Well Lieutenant I am going to retire, I have an important briefing with Admiral Mc'Kenzie in the morning," Michael said suppressing a sigh.

"Okay, I'll see ya' tomorrow cap'n."

With that, Kinraid watched the remainder of the outer colony news, while Michael returned to his quarters.

His new officer's quarters were located on deck 14, forward section of Delta base. They were considerably smaller than his previous family quarters; the deck his old quarters were located was still not fully repaired yet. However his new place was nicely laid out with a large comfortable bed, an opulent lounge and separate eating area.

Michael undressed, slid into bed, and settled down to his usual restless night's sleep.

The next morning arrived; he awoke, got dressed, had a small but appetizing breakfast, and headed to one of the myriad briefing rooms on the upper sections of the station to attend the briefing with Admiral Mc'Kenzie.

"Come in captain," The deep voiced admiral spoke.

Michael filed into the dimly lit briefing room; it was deceptively large an large oval table, lit and surrounded by chairs dominated the centre of the room, there was also a large viewer fixed to the far wall.

Michael saluted the man, who appeared to be in his mid forties with slightly greying hair, and sat down at the impressive table.

"How is your new second officer, Kinraid isn't it?"

"Yes admiral, he is proving to be an excellent officer sir," Michael replied, wondering what exactly the admiral was getting at.

"Good, because you'll need him, orders have just come through from E.D.F command; they are preparing a big push towards Gamma IV. The Krenarans in that area have not yet captured Echo base, but enemy ship numbers in that area have increased dramatically over the past few weeks. We think they are building for an attack on the base itself, and if it falls it could swing the entire war back in their favour."

Michael quickly realised the stakes were high; Echo base was the primary base for the engineering services. As well as the main shipyard for the navy; without it, repairs to naval vessels would be drastically cut as they would have to rely much more heavily on the smaller, less equipped substations. It also supplied a vast proportion of armoured support, arms and equipment to the Troop division.

"What kind of ground forces do they have there admiral?"

"The majority of the 3rd armoured company, the "Hells angels", as well as a sizeable proportion of the E.D.F Commandoes; led by your old buddy Colonel Vargev," The admiral smiled.

Michael chuckled a little, remembering his exploits with the enigmatic and notorious former Major Vargev.

"Something funny, captain?"

"Err...no sir, it's just I haven't heard from Colonel Vargev since just after we were both promoted together."

"The Liberty is cleared to depart at 18:00 hours with the sixth battlegroup, made up of the Jupiter class assault carrier Hermes, the

Danitza class battleships Defiant and Vengeance, four Jefferson class heavy destroyers......anyway the full fleet lists are on here."

The admiral passed him a disc for his data navigator, which he gently slid into a pocket on his uniform.

"However, you are to rendezvous with a second battlegroup at wolf 359, altogether there will be nearly two hundred E.D.F and Solarian ships taking part in this operation captain, and we expect heavy resistance......One last thing Solarian intelligence has picked up on this Krenaran."

The admiral pointed towards the viewer, it lit up showing the fuzzy image of a huge Krenaran, with heavy mechanical legs. His sheer size dwarfed the other Krenarans in the picture who, at eight feet tall, were not small either. "All we know is his name is Alax, and we think he is in command of the Krenaran military. The Solarians are scared stiff of this guy, and we believe he may be operating around Gamma IV. We have designated him an Alpha level threat, if we should locate him or find out which ship he is on, we are authorised to terminate with extreme prejudice. That will be all, Captain."

Michael saluted the admiral, and left the briefing room. Nearly two hundred ships, that's a hell of a lot of resources they are putting into one action, he thought.

Keying in a control on his wrist comm. Kinraids voice came over the device, "yes cap'n."

"Schedule a meeting for 14.00 hours commander, in one of the briefing halls. I want the whole crew there."

"Yes cap'n; is everythin' all right, sir?"

"We've got a new mission Quinn."

"I love it when ya' talk dirty cap'n."

Michael ended the communication with a chuckle as he continued down a long, brightly lit, curved corridor; towards the nearest elevator stop. Once it arrived he entered the large mass transit elevator.

After a few short minutes it stopped on his deck, and disgorged its payload of people, including Michael. Who hurried to his quarters and prepared his gear.

He packed a full landfall uniform, as well as his standard naval gear, carefully packing it all into a large black holdall.

After he finished packing, he reached into his pocket and took out the disc the admiral had given him, picked up his Data navigator from the glass table, and inserted the disc into it.

There was a detailed overview of the mission, the objectives, and a full list of the forces involved, he thumbed through it.

There were nearly seventy ships leaving from Delta base itself, another one hundred and thirty were stationed at Wolf 359. There were nearly eighty Solarian ships in the fleet alone.

He glanced over some of the names, the Nimitz, the Honduras, the Invincible, the Eurinades. These were some of the most famous ships in the fleet. By the time he had finished packing his gear and looked through the mission report, it was getting near 13.00 hours.

He decided to grab some lunch at a restaurant he had wanted to visit for some time on deck 11. As he made his way over to this restaurant, he could almost sense the station buzzing into life, it was always busy anyway; as a station of this size and importance invariably is, especially with the wartime repairs and the comings and goings of naval personnel.

However this felt different, it felt energized, as though something big was about to happen. Everywhere navy personnel could be seen loading supplies onto the multitude of vessels docked with the station.

Motorized carts and loading vehicles were busily transporting the heavier items onboard the enormous battleships, and servicing crews were performing systems checks and last minute repairs.

Michael was glad the Liberty was such a small vessel, at barely one hundred and forty meters long it didn't take nearly as long to prepare.

Briefings were shorter, since the standing crew of the Liberty was only 41 men. It could be prepped, briefed, and gone within an hour. The lumbering battleships and carriers needed nearly a full day.

However the downside to the Liberty was that although it is an E.D.F registered vessel; it was not built by the E.D.F. It was a captured Krenaran stealth ship, upgraded with Solarian weapons and technology. She is easily the fastest and arguably most deadly ship in the E.D.F fleet. However crewing her was a different matter entirely. Her systems were so far removed from standard E.D.F systems, that very few crewmen were actually able to operate them. This was the reason why Michael was placed in command of her, because it was he, and the then Major Vargev who captured her, and Michael who actually flew her.

He also wondered how much of the fleet had been upgraded with the new long range laser turrets. Since the older rail-cannons had proved to be utterly ineffective against Krenaran ships. Solarian scientists and the E.D.F research division had come up with the new designs, however to change the entire fleet over to the new weapon systems was taking time; and still only about a third of the E.D.F fleet were so equipped.

The pressure on the engineering services was huge, right across the entire E.O.C.A territory. The backlog was still several months until the change over was complete.

Michael arrived at the restaurant 'Wormholes end.' It was a large airy place, with lovely ambient lighting that danced across the walls, together with plants and even palm trees, giving the place an almost exotic, planet like feel; and situated within an orbital installation that was nearly one eighth the size of the moon. That was not an easy feat to achieve.

He ordered a large dinner, after having only a light breakfast, he was feeling very hungry. Quickly sitting down to eat, and taking a sip of coffee. He tended to prefer restaurants to the food synthesisers, because to him simply keying in a command and then taking your food, seemed terribly impersonal. He preferred the personal touch that being in a restaurant brings.

Once he had finished, he walked over to the payment area, and handed a rather fetching woman his payment card.

"Will that be all sir?" The long haired brunette woman asked.

"Yes, thank you." Handing her his payment card; the transaction was processed. The waitress handed it back to him.

"Thank you," he repeated; and then quietly left the restaurant.

His wrist comm. chirped, checking it he found it was from Kinraid. "I've managed to get briefing room 3, sir. If that's okay with ya', I've assembled the crew."

"Good work commander, I'm on my way," Michael replied, before closing the communication in mid-stride.

He arrived at the briefing hall, situated on deck 8, five minutes or so after 14.00 hours. He strode onto the small raised stage area in the centre of the hall. The room was laid out almost like a tiny old earth cinema, with an angled floor where people could all get a good view of the speaker.

The 40 other crewmembers which made up the crew of the Liberty all stood to attention as he entered.

"Please be seated."

The crew all sat quietly.

"As of this morning, we have new orders. We are to leave Delta base with the sixth battlegroup, and then join up with a second battlegroup, the 18th at Wolf 359. Once there we are ordered to advance to Gamma IV, and support the forces already there. We expect heavy resistance; reports suggest that Krenaran forces have been massing for an attack on Echo base itself. We are to ensure that doesn't happen, understood."

"Yes, Captain," The unanimous reply came.

"Any questions," Michael replied.

"What time do we depart sir?" Ensign Jackson asked.

"18.00 hours."

"How many ships will there be going on the mission sir?" Ensign Hawkins asked.

"All told, nearly two hundred."

There were shocked faces and audible gasps across the hall, 200 ships; it would be the biggest fleet action of the war so far.

"Would we get our usual pre battle drink, sir?" Lieutenant Jones asked with a wry smile.

It was an old naval custom that Michael re-introduced, although it only happened on board the Liberty. Before a mission, each crewman gets one measure of rum. It was something the admiralty didn't know about, but Michael found that it helped calm the crew, and relieved pre-battle nerves, and was something that the crew came to greatly appreciate.

"Yes, as always, one shot for each man; no more."

In unison, the crew threw up a great loud cheer.

"We get the ship prepped and ready first. Then the drink," Michael said as he dismissed the crew.

Later that day, the Liberty became a hive of activity, as supplies were brought aboard and loaded, systems checks were made, and the ship generally made ready to depart.

The chief weapons officer onboard, Lieutenant Logan Jones, ran through the various systems checks on the main fusion cannon with two tall Solarian assistants. He checked the magazines on the high energy torpedo launchers were full and the reactive hull armour was functioning properly. When he and the assistants were happy, they gave the weapons systems the all clear.

Eldathar, the Solarian navigation officer checked over all the thruster and pilot systems on board. Once this was complete he gave the piloting systems the all clear also.

Johnson Logameier, the ship's chief engineer checked over all the engineering systems with his accompanying Solarian assistants. Three quarters of the engineering staff were Solarian, and he found this frustrating at times. He checked over the plasma drive systems, sub-light engine, and the Solarian power core. After a slight re-calibration on one of the power feeds to the sub-light engine, he also gave the all clear.

Kathryn Jacobs, the only medical officer onboard, was busily stocking the small, rather rudimentary sickbay with appropriate medical supplies she had brought on board. There was no doubt in her mind she would need them, she always did on missions like this.

Michael and Quinn were busily checking over all the command functions, internal and external communications, the sensor suite and holographic viewscreen.

Once everybody was happy they all assembled in the command centre. All those checks and all that work had taken 57 minutes precisely to complete. Now the Liberty was ready for departure.

Michael went into his quarters, and contacted Admiral Mc'kenzie on the station, informing him that the Liberty was ready to get under way. Once the communication had ceased, he hefted a large bottle of rum out of an under-seat storage locker, and a tray full of shot glasses, before heading back out onto the command centre.

As he arrived back an expectant crew greeted him. Passing the rum to Quinn, he rested the tray of glasses on his own chair.

"As in the old navy tradition, 1 shot of rum each for the crew. May it warm your hearts before the coming of battle. Mr Kinraid, if you would like to pour the measures."

"Aye cap'n," he replied as he set about filling the glasses.

The crew formed a long queue around the periphery of the command centre, and Lieutenant Commander Kinraid poured each in turn 1 measure of rum. The crew refrained from drinking until all had a glass in their hand as per the ritual. Michael then lifted up his glass and exclaimed. "To the mission, and to victory!" he then promptly emptied his glass.

In unison the rest of the crew shouted, "to victory!" and together they all drank. Some drained their measure slowly, savouring the liquid, for they never knew if it would be their last taste. Others downed the rum in one gulp, hoping it would numb their senses to the horror that would most likely unfold.

Once the crew had finished, Kinraid collected the empty glasses and returned them to the tray. Michael then returned the bottle and the glasses back inside the storage locker in his quarters.

Kinraid then addressed the crew, "now 't' ya' stations."

The crew complied, and everyone took to their positions across the various decks of the ship.

Michael, upon returning to the command centre, took up his position in the famous centre seat. Kinraid took up the second officer's position at the sensory data console.

Michael pressed his wrist comm. "engineering, bring main power to maximum."

"Aye sir, bringing main power online." Logameier responded from engineering, simultaneously speaking into his wrist comm. and with his free hand, working the controls.

"Contact Delta base fleet command; request clearance to depart and join the fleet," Michael announced.

"Delta base responds, clearance is granted." Kinraid said as he turned in his seat to catch a last glimpse of the enormous naval installation, which apart from the Liberty was like a second home to him. It was largely repaired, though still the wounds of battle could be seen in certain areas. Small single man maintenance pods scoured over the damaged sections, like small ants constantly tending to a wounded giant. Men in environment suits also worked on the damaged sections. The flashes of their welding torches lit up the surrounding areas of space in tiny white bursts of light.

"Release the docking hatch."

With a whoosh of escaping air, the small hatch detached from the station with a dull metallic clunk, and slowly began to retract inside the one hundred and forty meter long, streamlined wedge shaped matt black and silver outer hull of the Liberty, where a panel slid over the exposed hatch, covering it and maintaining the ships stealth abilities at the same time.

"Main engines at ten percent reverse power, and thrusters at user's discretion." Michael said as he looked at the holographic viewscreen shimmering in front of the bridge crew. As the Liberty gradually reversed, thousands of viewports slowly became visible dotting the outer hull of the station, like tiny pin pricks of light across a vast metallic sea. A massive docking arm swung into view as Eldathar maneuvered the comparatively tiny ship underneath it. The lattice of girders, and pylons could clearly be seen. The Liberty continued reversing, and yet more of the station was revealed to the viewer. Its huge oval surface looked almost like a patchwork, some areas were newly repaired and the bright new metal shone with the light given off by passing ships and lights. Other areas still looked crumpled, blackened and scorched, where the repairs were still in progress.

Gradually, as the Liberty reversed yet more, the outer defence perimeter came into view, surrounding the station like a giant halo. This had taken the worst of the damage by the Krenarans, and large parts of it remained under repair. Nearly all of the giant rail-cannon turrets had been destroyed, as repairs continue they are to be replaced by the new high power, long range laser batteries.

Michael remembered when they first brought the Liberty to Delta base. A Solarian battlecruiser was on fire and adrift, out of control, the ship smashed through the perimeter. An entire section of the defence ring had given way under the impact, and even now a ragged, gaping hole was still there, a testament to the devastation.

The perimeter gradually receded as the Liberty continued to reverse, the flash of welding torches blinked across its entire structure.

At last Eldathar announced, "we are clear."

"Bring the ship about, and match formation with the fleet, bearing 160 elevation 2; One half sub-light."

"Yes captain," the softly spoken Solarian replied, his blue tinged skin flushing a slight shade of purple as he smiled.

The Liberty rapidly spun around, its powerful Solarian ionic thruster systems lit up a bright electric blue along the indented sides of the ship as it did so.

The negative ion propulsion system that was its main sub-light engine also glowed a similar colour as power was shunted to it.

Ahead of the small but lethal vessel, the silhouettes of the seventy or so ships loomed, all of them dwarfed the tiny Liberty as it made its way towards them. Massive lumbering Danitza class battleships came into view, their port and starboard sides lined with gigantic rail-cannons, their twin dorsal primary weapons turrets each one several times larger than the Liberty glinted in the light thrown out by the bright Orion sun, mingled with smaller, faster and far more advanced Solarian battlecruisers, their unmistakeable silver crescent shaped forms with their raised angular beak-like centre structures shone resplendently in the sunlight. Smaller, lighter Ghandhi class destroyers flitted between the larger ships taking up escort positions within the fleet.

At the head of this vast flotilla of ships, backlit against the Orion sun was the enormous wedge shape of a Jupiter class assault carrier, the largest ship in the entire E.D.F fleet. The shadows of the doors of its four large fighter bays gently indented into its dorsal hull were clearly visible, and together with its vast raised command superstructure all manner of complicated communications and tracking antennae extended out from the top of its structure like small silvery strands. Its raw size dwarfed everything around it, only the Danitza class battleships could hope to compare.

"The Hermes," Michael said quietly to himself, in awe of the almighty vessel and flagship of the flotilla. He had only ever seen one other throughout his entire career, and only four of these massive vessels were ever built.

"It must be one hell o' a fight if they're sending a Jupiter, cap'n," Kinraid said.

"Well they did say to expect heavy resistance," Michael replied, although he never imagined the scale of the battle that was to come.

The fleet grew in size as the Liberty neared, the small ship deftly flew under the massive, rectangular hull of a hulking Danitza class, and up over the shape of a Jefferson class heavy destroyer, the running lights of its communications and sensor towers reflected dimly off the dark matt black hull of the Liberty, just for an instant turning it a slight shade of green, and then red in colour as the lights blinked.

Finally, it took up a position somewhere in the middle of the fleet, amongst some Alexander class medium cruisers that; although they were nowhere near the size of the battleships or carriers of the fleet, still dwarfed the small Liberty.

There they waited for the all clear to commence operations, everyone on the command centre of the Liberty all looked towards the viewscreen, seeing only the aft and giant turbines of the inter-system boosters of the multitude of ships in front of them.

The viewscreen switched to the form of a dark haired, bearded man of Japanese descent. "This is Admiral Takeda Sato of the Hermes to the fleet, clearance has been given, prepare to enter plasma drive matching speed and course."

The image of the man quickly swapped to the view of the fleet ahead as the communication ended.

"You heard the man," Michael said.

Slowly but surely, the entire fleet fired their inter-system boosters, building up speed before unleashing a multitude of charged plasma beams from their forward plasma emitters. The positively and negatively charged plasma energy beams collided with one another, releasing tremendous bursts of energy in the form of a cacophony of bright white flashes that even lit up delta base now far in the distance.

The swirling multi-hued plasma wakes opened up in front of each vessel, surrounded by a fringe of bright white light as the fleet careered towards them at full speed. As the multitude of vessels entered the plasma wakes the energy collapsed in on themselves in an equally blinding flash, lighting up delta base once again, and leaving nothing but the starry blackness of deep space, the fleet had now shifted into plasma drive, and hurtled toward their destination.

2. A gathering of power.

Michael Alexander studied the viewscreen, taking in the grey silhouettes of the E.D.F ships, and the sleek metallic crescent shaped hulls of the Solarian ones. All surrounded by the swirling reds, blues, and purple colours of the plasma wake that they were using to travel through space much faster than the speed of light.

He knew that in comparison, the Liberty and the Solarian ships were travelling very slowly, only at plasma factor 3, which was all that the larger and far slower Hermes and the other E.D.F ships could manage, since they had far less advanced plasma drive systems than they had.

In truth the Liberty had a top speed of plasma factor 7, over twice as fast as any E.D.F ship, and the fast and powerful Solarian battlecruisers could even manage plasma factor 9.

Later that night, Michael went off duty and retired to his quarters. On his desk lay several systems status reports that required his attention. Walking over to the food synthesiser on the far wall, he keyed in a request for a latté from the touch screen menu system, and then sat down to pore over the reports.

He had chose Ensign Jeffrey Hawkins to be in command during the nightshift, since the young ensign was soon to go through his bridge officers training, prior to his push for promotion to lieutenant as a sensory specialist. Michael thought the experience might do him some good.

The door opened, and in stepped Kinraid. "Do ya' mind, if I have a word with ya' cap'n."

"No, not at all commander, come, have a seat," Michael motioned to an empty chair by the side of his desk. "Would you like a drink, I've just ordered one."

"No thank you," Kinraid replied as he sat down, brushing his long auburn locks as he did so. "it's tha' crew sir, I think they 'r' a little nervous, so they are. This is the biggest fleet action in tha' history of the E.D.F, the crew have only been working together for seven months, and I have only been here a month myself."

"I know everyone is a little edgy commander, hell so am I, and I have no idea how it is going to turn out or even if we'll make it back." He rose from his desk and walked towards the viewport, pointing a finger out to the ships gliding alongside. "There are seventy other ships out there, feeling exactly the same as we are, some of them don't have the benefit of reactive hull armour and fusion cannon that we do. They have wives and families too, all they can do is dive right into the lions den and hope to god they come back out alive. We all have to have faith in one another commander."

Kinraid paused to consider this for a moment, "thank ya' captain, I hope the poor souls on those other ships do make it back."

"So do I."

The next few days went largely without incident; Michael toured the ship as he usually did when there was not a great deal to do. Always marvelling at some new piece of technology that he didn't know was there. The Liberty wasn't just an ordinary ship to him; it was more like his home and his friend. With this ship they had helped overturn the whole Krenaran war, this tiny little vessel and he had fought and bled together. If it was even possible for ships to bleed, he felt as though the Liberty was almost an extension of himself.

He visited engineering, checking if everything was okay there, even managing to help Lieutenant Logameier cure a slight problem with the secondary transjectors, which smoothed the flow of Ions into the negative Ion propulsion drive. Michael hadn't the faintest idea how it worked, this was all Solarian technology and radically advanced to him. It was a good job we had those Solarian assistants onboard, he thought.

Over the course of the next few hours, they neared the Wolf 359 system.

Michael had made his way to the centre of the bridge, waiting for word from the Hermes to drop out of plasma drive, after about ten minutes or so, the holographic viewscreen automatically shimmered into existence.

"Hermes to the fleet, prepare to drop out of plasma drive on my order."

Michael nodded to Kinraid.

"Liberty confirms," the commander spoke into his station.

"Prepare to drop out of plasma drive in one minute," the face of Sato addressed the fleet.

Exactly one minute later, the entire flotilla dropped out of plasma drive together with a gigantic blinding flash; their inter-system boosters blazed into life and the fleet gradually accelerated toward the other battlegroup that awaited them.

Michael had begun to get a bad feeling in his stomach, over the course of the past few months he had learned to trust that feeling. It had kept him alive on more than one occasion.

"See if you can get me a visual on that second battlegroup commander."

Kinraid flew into action, his fingers working the console, "sure cap'n, here ya' are."

Sure enough, there was the source of Michaels' bad feeling. In the distance he could see the faint tiny shapes of the ships that made up the other battlegroup. However, distant flashes of far off explosions could also be made out, like the faint twinkling of starlight, blinking into and out of existence all around the other fleet, faint blue traces of fusion cannon beams were barely perceptible in the dark starlit backdrop of deep space. The battlegroup was under heavy attack.

"Hermes to the fleet; advance attack speed, and engage." The voice of Admiral Takeda Sato rang out through the speakers.

On the viewer, Krenaran stealth ships could be seen rapidly darting into and out of the battlegroup performing attack runs, like hungry barracudas picking off stragglers. Their sleek, angular wedge shaped hulls almost identical to the Liberties own, minus the plethora of upgraded systems, with their dark matt-black colouring interspersed with silvery metallic panels. Towards the rear of the tightly packed mass of vessels, the flaming broken hull of an Alexander class medium cruiser listed. Explosions continued to rip through the shattered vessels hull.

Jesus, Michael thought, they are like a pack of fucking wolves. "Order battlestations, bring reactive hull armour online and boost power to the fusion cannon, and torpedo launchers."

Virtually as he was saying it, the command centre became a hive of activity as the veteran crew of the Liberty carried out his orders with speed and precision, lights dimmed, giving the room a menacing air, an alarm gently rang out, indicating the ship was at maximum readiness. The reactive hull armour crackled as a faint blue shimmer ran through the dark outer hull of the ship. The awesomely powerful Solarian fusion cannon powered up, with its customary low pitched 'thoom' noise. The Liberty was now ready for battle.

The viewscreen shimmered into existence once again, "6th battlegroup, break and attack."

The Liberty and the accompanying Solarian elements of the fleet, shot forward, easily outpacing the rest of the E.D.F battlegroup, thanks to their far more powerful thruster systems.

The massive Hermes hung back, co-ordinating the rest of the fleet, and made ready to disgorge its waves of fighters and bombers it had placed on hot standby, when the time was right.

The huge, hulking Danitza's, ponderously manoeuvred their great size to bring their awesome weapon systems to bear. While the smaller, more agile Ghandhi class destroyers and Mandela class light cruisers sped forward into the assault.

Some of the Alexander class medium cruisers hung back to form up as escorts, helping protect the larger ships from attack themselves. The accompanying Jefferson class heavy destroyers although barely a third of the size of a Danitza added their considerable firepower to the fray, their specially designed rotary rail-cannons although much smaller than the battleships allow them to get in close and literally pound the enemy to pieces, some of them had gone through the upgrade process, changing their rail-cannons for the Solarian based high power lasers, as rail-cannon shells proved so ineffective against Krenaran shipping during the onset of the war.

3. Prelude to Armageddon.

The Liberty surged forward as Eldathar rapidly banked the ship to avoid the incoming particle cannon fire from several enemy Krenaran ships directly ahead of them.

Liberty, and the other Solarian battlecruisers traded fire with their own fusion cannons. Multiple incandescent blue energy beams shot forth from the Solarian reinforcements, their raw power instantly decimating three of the Krenaran vessels in bright balls of flame.

Behind them, the Danitza class battleships Defiant and Vengeance; recently upgraded with the new long range laser turrets opened fire, deep blue energy beams from their massive primary dorsal turrets lanced out across space and smashed into two more of the Krenaran ships. One was hit amidships; a ragged flaming hole marked the impact site on the vessel. The other was hit directly in its rear engines, which detonated violently, blasting apart half the ship, the fiery debris strewn wreckage spun out of control.

Four more Krenaran ships rapidly swooped in to perform an attack run on another Danitza, its accompanying escorts firing volley after volley, trying to shoot down the attackers. However they were proving to be elusive targets.

The Liberty changed course to intercept, "target the closest ship, fire torpedoes when ready," Michael said.

Two high energy torpedoes sped towards one of the Krenaran ships, they were elusive but not enough to outwit the advanced guidance systems of the Liberties torpedoes. They detonated upon impact and tore apart the Krenaran ship in a devastating fireball.

Long range laser fire from the Hermes' own comparatively limited batteries had managed to annihilate two more of the stealth ships, while the last remaining Krenaran vessel abandoned its attack run.

On the viewer, through the fiery debris of destroyed Krenaran stealth ships and the explosions of battle, Michael could just about make out the shape of a far larger Krenaran ship beginning to form, the massive flat topped vessel had a huge command structure located towards the rear of the gigantic ship. Michael's heart sank as the sight filled him with dread, he had seen these ships before in news reports, but never actually encountered one. They were the Krenaran command carriers, the largest and most deadly ships in the Krenaran fleet, and he was all too aware of the firepower one of these ships possessed.

Solarian intelligence briefings had told the E.D.F that the small rectangular pods which slowly rose close to the fore of the flat main hull contained rapid firing H.O.T rockets, which worked on Heat Ordnance Tracking. The E.D.F navy had a database of all enemy ships encountered thus far in its history, and each was listed according to the threat it represented, this was known as its threat level.

Michael remembered that this ship was listed as an alpha level threat, the highest threat level that can be given to a ship.

The H.O.T rocket, was a type of torpedo that homed in on any given heat signature on any ship that didn't display a correct Krenaran I.F.F signature.

Michael remembered that it was these ships that were responsible for the decimation of unarmed refugee transports around the Aurelias colony nearly eight months ago, ending almost ten thousand lives in barely five minutes.

Now the huge Krenaran command carrier advanced, slowly, menacingly toward the fleet as those deadly rectangular pods began to rise once again.

The remaining stealth ships all retreated towards it consolidating their position; some were caught and decimated by Solarian fusion cannons and E.D.F lasers.

However, the Krenaran carrier had not yet launched its waves of attack craft, interesting, Michael thought.

Instead those rectangular pods gradually rose to their full height, and with a dull metallic 'clunk' locked into place.

He knew that even the Liberty with all its speed and agility would never make it to that carrier before it launched its deadly payload. They would have to brace themselves for the inevitable onslaught that the enemy ship would unleash upon them before trying for a counter attack.

There was a deathly silence, as the crew of the Liberty looked on through the shimmering viewscreen with fear in their eyes, as if they were staring death in the face, for none of them knew when the command carrier would launch its deadly payload, or even if they would be hit or not. If they were, the Liberty would most likely not withstand it.

Six intensely bright flashes lit up the forward hull of the enemy carrier in quick succession as it unleashed the missiles. The multiple warheads sped towards them with incredible speed.

As the warheads hurtled towards them, the remainder of the Krenaran fleet leapt into plasma drive, and were gone. The multiple H.O.T rockets continued to speed towards the E.D.F fleet, ships opened fire attempting to shoot down the onrushing torpedoes to no avail, they were just too fast to get a lock on. Michael could just make out the blazing white flare of the enemy missiles engine.

Before they could hardly blink, a Ghandhi class destroyer burst apart in flames as one of the torpedoes smashed into it dead centre with horrific force. The destroyer was stationed right next to the Liberty, and the tiny ship shuddered violently from the force of the explosion. People were thrown to the floor, consoles across the ship shattered, sending sparks showering. Smoke filled the command centre as delicate electronics ruptured and sizzled, and it was all Michael could do just to hang onto his seat.

Eldathar had managed to hang on and flung the ship into a steep dive as the mid section of the devastated destroyer hurtled towards them wreathed in flame. It shot past missing slamming into the Liberties rear engines by a matter of only a few feet.

There was carnage in the rest of the fleet where the torpedoes struck home. Two of the missiles slammed into the Battleship Achilles, who the Liberty had just helped to save, turning its enormous rear engines into flaming ruins.

Two other torpedoes blasted apart a Mandela class light cruiser as well as an Alexander class medium cruiser both ships tore themselves to pieces as their reactor cores ruptured, sending debris careering in all directions. The final torpedo decimated a Jefferson class heavy destroyer, the ship listed lazily as fire swept through the vesel, before it too burst apart in a bright fireball.

The tightly packed mass of ships weaved to and fro trying to avoid the maelstrom of destroyed vessels and debris; several ships almost collided into one another in their rush to escape the onslaught. Only the skill of the pilots prevented an even bigger disaster.

When the chaos had finally subsided, Michael asked for a full status report.

"We have some small electrical fires on deck four; deck six had taken some damage from th' explosion cap'n, and a few minor scrapes, but all in all, we are not in bad shape all things considered; not in bad shape at all." Kinraid replied, his thick Irish accent showing through.

"Good, have repair crews tackle the fires, and begin repairs."

"Already done sir."

It was to be expected, Michael thought, though if Eldathar hadn't reacted with the speed that he did, we would have all been gonners for sure. When he saw the flaming wreckage of that Ghandhi class destroyer hurtling toward him, his life had flashed before his eyes.

The casualty rate had been higher than he had expected however, they had lost twelve ships in total, four of them were Solarian. Those delicate crescent shaped metallic craft now floated uncontrollably, their slender hulls fractured and broken. The Achilles had taken severe damage and was on fire on several decks, it could no longer take part in the larger battle at Gamma IV.

Instead it would have to limp toward Delta Foxtrot base, a small naval facility on the edge of the wolf 359 system. It was a heavy blow, the

Danitza's brought a lot of firepower to the table and losing one, meant losing all that weaponry.

The rest of the 6th battlegroup formed up with this second fleet, and together the remaining 188 vessels all leapt into plasma drive, a huge burst of light erupted as they did so. The other damaged vessels would have to make what repairs they could along the way.

It was another three day journey to Gamma IV, and Michael knew that this little skirmish was but a small taste of what awaited them when they arrived. He felt decidedly uneasy about the prospect.

The Krenarans now knew that they were coming, word would have spread from those escaped ships, and there was no way E.D.F command could have prevented a build up of ships of this magnitude to go unseen anyway, the attack was but a small skirmish designed to thin out the numbers a little, before the main battle.

As they continued on their journey towards the planet, Michael spent much of his time going through the repair reports of the damage suffered at the hands of the Krenaran attack. The damage to deck six, was a little more serious than they had first thought. Debris from the destroyed Ghandhi class destroyer had, in places, caused minute fractures in the hull, as debris fragments collided against it; possibly weakening the Liberties stealth abilities. All Michael could do was wait and see, it could not be fixed in transit, that's for sure.

4. A desperate defence.

Colonel Nikolai Vargev was stood on a concrete platform at the top of the main command tower high above the surrounding buildings and workshops within Echo base. Silently looking out over the windswept plains of Gamma IV and stroking his dark moustache. It was a bleak, cold, often damp place. Raising his binoculars he could see the shadowy forms of the Valcasian mountains on the horizon, and the glinting steel structures of the far off colony buildings in between, the bright sunlight of the Gamma sun shining off them.

The shipyards and naval repair stations were all in orbit above the planet, while the vast tank factories, munitions factories and warehouses were on the surface itself.

Vargev squinted through his binoculars, gently panning them across the horizon, straining to catch any glimpse of the advancing Krenaran ground forces. He didn't know how many there were, but he knew they were coming. He had sent two squads of his most expert trackers to ascertain the size of the enemy forces almost six hours earlier, he was confident they would return; as yet they hadn't.

General John Steel; the British commander of the 3rd armoured company, the 'Hells angels,' strode up and stood next to the big Russian.

"Still wondering where the devil they are colonel?"

"Something like that," Vargev smiled as he continued to peer into the binoculars.

The platform they stood upon, was atop a twelve story high tower, the other floors all contained training rooms, workshops for aspiring E.D.F engineers, as well as offices for the hundreds of operations staff of the base itself.

To his north, lay the 40 feet high, reinforced concrete perimeter wall, and the guard towers which studded it in even intersections, directly ahead of them was the main gate, where the two largest guard towers loomed over a wide tarmac road, serving as the only entrance into the base. A giant barrier and security station barred access, which could only be opened by inputting a unique identification code issued to all staff working on the base.

To Vargev's west, there stood the massive munitions factories, where tonnes of rail-cannon shells, and a host of other ammunition was made, and even further to the west, he could just make out the tops of the enormous tank factories, huge columns of steam rose from their stacks from the cooling processes used to make the armour.

Running through the middle of those tank factories was a narrow yet deep canal, which provided the vast quantities of water used; named the Aquarius canal by the workers after the astrological water carrier.

As Vargev turned his attentions eastward, he could see the vast shape of the spaceport, several hundred meters wide. It was designed to accommodate the bulk freighters who would transfer tanks, other armoured vehicles and supplies to larger freighters in orbit which would in-turn transport them to whichever E.O.C.A colony was in need of them.

Attached to the spaceport was the even bigger loading area, where vehicles would be arrayed for each particular pickup, then driven onto the freighters themselves.

Further east, Vargev cast his eye over the tall warehouse buildings, where tanks and equipment would be stored awaiting pickup. It was always busy around those buildings as military vehicles drove to and fro from the loading area.

As he returned his attention northwards once again, he could make out the snaking course of the river Tariseia, where the Aquarius canal got its water. It ran through Gamma colony, about a few kilometres further up the road. The colony itself was a small self contained city, built for the workers at echo base.

Vargev knew he should feel comfortable in the formidable protection that Echo base offered, but he didn't. There would be an attack soon, he could feel it, but hadn't a clue where the attack would come from, the tension was rising amongst the men, as it always did on the eve of battle.

As he looked over the base in front of him, he could just make out a lone soldier, playing on an old antique harmonica to others around him, the Russian smiled.

The E.D.F naval vessels that were posted to this area were pushed almost to breaking point trying to hold back the Krenaran attackers. However, sooner or later a Krenaran force will break through, capture the shipyard and then launch an all out attack upon the surface. Every instinct within him was telling him this, and he trusted those instincts, they had kept him alive.

Vargev had barely a hundred E.D.F commandoes under his command, the most highly trained and deadly troops in the E.D.F. Used in the fiercest of the fighting, each man was already a veteran of a dozen engagements during this war, every one a perfectly honed killing machine.

He had posted them to strategic locations where he knew the fighting would be thickest. The spaceport, and dug in within the colony itself. The spaceport would be a high priority for the Krenarans as they would no doubt use it as a staging post to spread out and attack the rest of the base, two twelve man squads lay in wait there to prevent that happening, with their lives if necessary.

The rest; apart from another two squads which were held back to defend the command building itself were ordered to fan out amongst the buildings of the colony, and to prevent the Krenarans from capturing it in the hopes of laying siege to the base itself.

General Steel however, had far more resources at his disposal. He had bolstered the commandoes position at the spaceport with four Apollo main battle tanks, and two dominator assault walkers.

Most of his heavy armour was placed amongst the warehouse buildings and within gamma colony, whereas the faster moving elements of the company he had set up in the Valcasian mountains, as a large pass ran straight through them.

Vargev had approved of the generals decision of sending the 14 or so dominators to gamma colony, as their rugged survivability, thick armour and firepower made them excellent units to use in a built up area, where their comparative slowness wasn't an issue. Together with 6 more Apollo tanks dug in within the colony, it was pretty well defended.

However, he had staunchly disagreed with Steel's decision of sending the large force of raider A.T.V's and rapier light tanks up into the mountains, as Vargev thought the attack was unlikely to come from there, enemy units would have to cover large areas of open ground once clear of the mountains, leaving them vulnerable. However the general had overruled him to his chagrin.

The hot Gamma sun had settled below the horizon, bringing nightfall to the colony. The stars glittered in the inky blackness overhead, and the faint clicks of men checking their weapons could be heard through the quiet night air.

Vargev could pick up the faint, barely audible conversations of the lesser trained infantry sharing soldier stories, he silently harrumphed at their lack of discipline, at giving their positions away so easily. His commandoes however were all perfectly silent. Quietly watching, and waiting. Vargev smiled to himself in pride, before allowing himself to rest briefly before the fireworks began.

Lieutenant Shaw was stood on guard at the main gate when he heard a faint dull whine passing overhead. Glancing around his immediate area, he could see nothing.

Two other soldiers, Corporal Jackson and Sergeant Forrest were busily playing poker. Trying to pass the time until their guard shift ended.

The whining grew steadily louder; Shaw, now troubled by the noise shone his torch over the dark surroundings, but still could not perceive anything of significance. Readying his pulse rifle just in case, he gave out a blind call of "Halt, who goes there. Identify yourself."

No reply came.

At this call, the two other soldiers put down their cards, and headed over to Shaw's position. "What's up Lieutenant, you seem kinda jumpy tonight, your shadow scaring you again?" Forrest asked jokily.

"Just thought I heard something, a faint whine passing near; probably nothing."

"Could be the munitions factories," Jackson offered.

"Could be," Shaw nodded in agreement. "Keep your eyes open anyway."

A much louder whine appeared to shoot past them, followed by such a powerful blast of air that it nearly blew the three of them off their feet.

"What the hell!" Forrest shouted.

They shone their torches skywards and could just about make out the matt-black and silver metallic hulls that marked the underside of the dreaded Krenaran stealth ships; barely visible in the dark night sky.

"Shit it's the Krenarans!" Jackson yelled.

"Get command on the line; now!" Shaw ordered, as he barely finished his sentence the guard tower across the road burst into flames as a torpedo smashed into it and blew it apart, showering the three of them in concrete dust and debris. The flames lit up the main gate in a bright orange glow, and smoke billowed out into the night sky.

The commotion forced Vargev awake with a start, and he ran to one of the forward windows in the upper floors of the command building. He could see the orange glow of the flames and the thick black smoke of the destroyed guard tower billowing out high into the night sky.

"I fucking knew it; the Krenarans must have captured the shipyard." He said to himself as he grabbed his trusty Armschlager .44 caliber heavy machine gun, and sprinted down to meet up with Steel and the rest of the command team on the 8th floor of the building.

A flare was launched from near the main gate, high into the sky. It light illuminated the dark silhouettes of the stealth ships passing by overhead, as well as those that had already landed unseen, disgorging hundreds of Krenaran warriors between them. Those which had already landed their payload of troops began to lift off ready for the attack on the base itself.

Two more Krenaran ships swooped in low, firing their powerful bright green particle beams at the perimeter fence in a deafening roar, blasting away huge chunks of scorched concrete.

Vargev rushed into the makeshift command centre, just as another officer shouted, "they are attacking the fence!"

Another Krenaran ship swooped in, unleashing a torpedo straight at the fourth floor, the missile smashed through a conference window and detonated, blasting apart the entire floor in the fury of the explosion. Glass shattered and flames burst from the damaged floor as smoke billowed out, the entire building shook from the force of the explosion.

Vargev and the rest of the command team were thrown to the ground, gradually they got back to their feet, brushing themselves down.

Cannons in the guard towers began returning fire with a deafening chattering roar, as their tracer fire streaked across the night sky, however the Krenaran ships were too fast and too agile and few shots actually hit.

The few Hellfire anti-air units they possessed also opened fire. Their rapid firing heavy laser turrets lit up the night sky in intense flashes of blue energy. The stealth abilities of the Krenaran ships however confused their targeting systems and most of the shots went astray, one however was caught and hit repeatedly, the craft slammed into the ground on the far side of the colony, smoke and flames billowing out from the twisted wreckage.

Vargev ran to where Steel was stood, "we need to get out of this building, fast."

"I hope the rear emergency exits are still intact. Everyone with me, we're evacuating."

Steel, Vargev and around twenty other troops all ran for the exits, when they got there, they found the emergency escape ladders were damaged but still usable.

"Move!" The big Russian shouted over the noise of battle outside.

They quickly began to make their way down the steel steps, as a second torpedo slammed into the front of the building with a deafening explosion, violently shaking the tower once again. Vargev and Steel clung on desperately, but another soldier wasn't so lucky, as the force of the shaking unbalanced him and sent him plummeting over the side of the steps, landing with a sickening crunch seven floors below.

Overhead Vargev could just make out the shapes of three more stealth ships incoming from west to east, as they swooped down, they unleashed a salvo of torpedoes. A hellfire anti-air battery was hit, the force of the impact blasting the near 30 tonne vehicle almost ten feet into the air. The wreckage came crashing down in flames, scattering razor sharp debris.

More shots rained down upon Echo base, blasting a wide hole in a tank factory roof, another torpedo decimated the top floor of the command tower, where Vargev had earlier stood.

Elsewhere another guard tower burst into flames as it too was hit, sending the occupants plummeting on fire, to the ground below.

Vargev, and the surviving troops had made it to ground level and quickly began to take stock of their situation. Chaos was everywhere, two guard towers were burning, and the command building was now thoroughly ablaze after taking several hits, like a giant pyre in the centre of the base.

Luckily the munitions factories had been spared, if they had been hit, with all those explosives inside. The resultant blast could take out half the base.

Amongst the flashes of torpedo fire, anti-air fire and tracer shots, two bulk freighters began to descend bearing E.D.F markings, they hovered low, as though attempting to land on the spaceport. The freighters held position barely two meters from the surface of the pad.

Vargev eyed the transports with suspicion, why the hell are the Krenarans ignoring those transports? Almost in an instant the realization hit him; holy shit!

A hatch opened on both freighters, dozens of Krenarans poured out of the hovering vessels. Their weapons mercilessly scything down the E.D.F troops attempting to stop them landing.

The freighters eventually touched down on the landing pad, releasing a second wave of warriors, their weapons blazing away.

Vargev cast a glance northwards and could see yet more Krenaran ships landing in the dusty fields between Echo base and the colony. This is not going to be a fucking good night.

For the most part, the perimeter fence was holding up to the onslaught, the reinforced concrete was doing its job well. However it wouldn't last too much longer, already in several places it was cracked and broken.

At the main gate, a dozen or so soldiers were hurriedly forming a barricade.

Vargev sprinted towards the loading area connected to the spaceport. The surviving soldiers there had managed to close one of the sliding heavy steel doors, and were trying to fortify it with anything they could find.

Just outside the building, he could hear the unmistakable 'thump' 'thump', of the heavy footfalls of dominator assault walkers. Two of them were approaching, Vargev rushed back out and signalled to the pilots, who turned their metal behemoths and began to follow.

"I want you two to guard that door!" he shouted up to them, "any Krenaran that comes through I want dead."

The two pilots nodded their understanding. Taking up positions near the door, their multi-barreled heavy assault cannons trained upon it.

Loud metallic 'clangs' resounded across the hushed loading area. As fire from Krenaran weaponry slammed against the heavy steel on the opposite side.

Vargev and the remainder of the commandoes readied their weapons.

Powerful explosions continued to light up the night sky outside as stealth ships maintained their assault on the base.

Apollo main battle tanks were directed towards the main gate to provide a defence to the inevitable attack there.

In the distance, General Steel could see multiple explosions lighting up Gamma colony, the black shapes of Krenaran ships silhouetted against the glow of fires swooping in and out, performing strafing runs. He knew however that it was just a diversion to get the forces he had placed there to keep their heads down so they can land more men.

He motioned to a young soldier nearby.

"Yes sir."

"Where's your comm. unit," the General asked.

"Here sir," the young soldier pulled out the comm. unit out of a pouch on his webbing, and passed it over to Steel.

He input the frequency to contact the forward command post in the Valcasian mountains, "This is General Steel to all units, Echo base is under attack, all units are ordered to return to Echo base; repeat return to base."

He passed the soldier his comm. unit back, and looked out beyond the main gate towards the hundreds of Krenarans massing for the attack, barely half a kilometre away.

I just hope some of those units make it here, he thought. Another explosion from the burning command centre nearby made him duck.

The main body of the Krenaran force did not advance however, instead they dug themselves in. Knowing they could not yet penetrate the thick outer perimeter. Instead the Stealth ships renewed their attacks, bombarding the base throughout the night.

When the sun arose on the second day, barely two of the guard towers were still standing and smoke hung thick in the air. The Krenarans were well dug in, in the fields between Gamma colony and Echo base.

The burned out command tower still smouldered, though now barely better than ruins. The first rainfall the colony had seen in nearly 3 months gradually began to patter off the armour of the Apollo's and the Dominator's.

Barely a quarter of the raider A.T.V's and Rapier light tanks had made it back from the Valcasian mountains during the night, their blackened twisted chassis could be seen dotting the fields close to the Krenaran lines, wisps of light smoke could still be seen from some of them.

Steel had ordered the Groundhog artillery batteries to remain within the mountains, and co-ordinate their fire with the two other batteries positioned within Echo base, they continuously pounded the Krenaran lines with high velocity shells.

An emergency field hospital was set up during the night in one of the tank factories, and was rapidly filling up with the injured and dying.

Engineers from within Echo base itself were hurriedly trying to shore up the perimeter fence before the attacks resumed again.

Vargev joined Steel, near the main gate. "Well, we made it through the night," the general said.

"We may well have to make it through more yet comrade."

In the distance they could see the faint wisps of smoke rising from the colony.

"How many casualties?" Vargev asked.

"70 dead all told, nearly twice that many injured," Steel replied with a sigh.

"Not bad considering the beating we took."

"Yes, but not good either. I've been a fool colonel, I almost allowed the Krenarans to waltz right in through the front door. Most of the faster units, the Raiders and the Rapiers were left well out of position, you were right to tell me not to put the majority of my forces in the mountains."

"What is done, is done comrade, what we have to do now is hold the base until help arrives; at all costs."

"The stealth ships won't attack during the day that's for sure."

"One of the biggest problems we have is how the hell do we re-capture the spaceport?" Vargev asked rubbing his soot streaked chin.

The commander of Echo base General Kalidis approached the two men.

"Where the bloody hell were you during the attack!" Steel shouted.

"Cut off; I was in the far tank factory when the attack came. I know of a small entrance to the roof of the loading area, I'll show you."

He led them over to the front of the loading platform near to the perimeter fence itself, it was partially covered by foliage. But there was a very small flight of slippery, rusted steel steps that led up onto the roof.

Vargev and Steel climbed up the steps, peering over the roofline, they could make out the Krenarans were busily assembling something. Neither of them had any idea what it was. They were milling about the freighters, going back and forth, bringing out equipment. One massive Krenaran strode into view, standing upon a pair of thick mechanical legs, he was head and shoulders above the others and almost seemed to exude a sense of raw power, he bellowed out orders to the others around him.

Vargev ducked back down, remembering back to the time six months ago when they fought Axus on the bridge of the Liberty, the one who had almost killed Vargev himself. "You must be presented as trophies for my master," he had said to them at the devastated Agemman colony before taking them both prisoner. Could this be the one, could this be the master that Axus had spoken of; he certainly looked bigger than Axus, that's for sure, and appeared stronger.

Steel looked over at the colonel, "are you okay, you look like you've seen a ghost."

"I'm fine," Vargev lied.

"Who is that?" Steel asked as he also eyed the huge Krenaran working and directing those around him, typical Krenarans had a single barrel arm cannon, a weapon that was physically grafted onto the Krenarans own arm and was immensely powerful. However this guy's weapon had not one, but three barrels.

"I've no idea, all I know is that Axus once called him his master."

The massive Krenaran looked over in their direction and spotted them at once; levelling his weapon he opened fire, three intensely bright green translucent beams hurtled towards them, Vargev and steel barely managed to duck back down as the shot blasted apart a section of concrete next to them, covering the both of them in choking dust, and showering them in masonry.

"Jesus Christ, that weapon is a hell of a lot more powerful than the typical Krenaran weapons!" Steel shouted over the noise of the blast.

"You're telling me, time to get out of here," Vargev replied.

They made their way back down the rusted steps, disappearing from view of the Krenarans.

During the rest of the day, they had moved all of the Apollo main battle tanks, and the majority of the dominator assault walkers towards the perimeter fence. Vargev could almost feel that the Krenarans would make a push for it tonight, try and break through the perimeter to join up with their other force on the spaceport.

The remaining commandoes; Vargev had ordered into fire teams, taking up positions on the warehouse rooves, near to the perimeter, where their powerful, heavy calibre Armschlagers would tear into the approaching Krenarans.

The commandoes that had fallen back from the space port, regrouped in the loading area, taking up new positions amongst the parked vehicles. Vargev had elected to allow them to stay, in case the Krenarans did manage to break through that enormous steel door that separated the loading area from the rest of the space port.

The Sun of Gamma IV was beginning to set, and night would soon be upon them. General Steel would be leading the defence of the main gate, while Vargev together with the other commandoes would be defending the perimeter. Kalidis would be out saving his own ass again, Vargev thought, he had taken an instant dislike to that man.

The sky had darkened noticeably and night time was fast upon them, it had been steadily raining all day, now it was getting gradually heavier. Vargev took up his position near to the perimeter. The rain had formed small rivulets down his helmet; he offered a silent prayer that he would see the night through.

The rain continued to patter off the helmets and camouflaged fatigues of the dug in commandoes as they silently awaited the coming attack, their weapons had all been checked and were ready for the inevitable onslaught that was to come.

The soft, low pitched hum of approaching stealth ships signalled the resumption of the attacks, just as they had done the previous night. Several of the deadly craft swooped down towards the base, unleashing a salvo of torpedoes as they did so, some of which smashed into the perimeter fence, blasting out gigantic pieces of concrete and masonry.

Another shot tore apart an Apollo M.B.T which was defending the main gate. Its flaming wreckage was sent tumbling end-over-end before smashing into the ruined guard tower. The roar of the hellfire anti-air batteries resounded across the complex as they once again tried to halt the swooping stealth ships, but as yet to no avail.

The Krenaran ships dived to the attack along gamma colony also, their torpedoes and particle cannons tearing apart the tightly packed structures; great plumes of fire and smoke rose high into the night air.

Casualties however had remained light in the initial attacks so far, as the majority of vehicles and men had dug in, or taken cover in or around the buildings for better protection.

The stealth ships swung around in a high arc, to resume their pounding of the perimeter fence once again; explosions lit up the night sky in bright flashes as torpedoes struck home. Throughout the assault Krenaran ground forces were steadily advancing towards the perimeter. Heavy weapons fire from the two remaining guard towers raked the advancing Krenarans, cutting them down as they approached, dozens of the green scaled draconic brutes fell clutching holes the size of fists in their chests.

The Krenaran ground troops were now almost within weapons range. The mighty Apollo's opened fire with deafening blasts from their cannons, the high velocity rounds throwing up great plumes of charred earth and smoke where the rounds detonated. Several dozen of the aliens were blasted high into the air by the force of the impacts, heedless of their losses the brutal Krenarans continued to advance.

A lone stealth ship opened fire with its particle cannon at one of the guard towers a few feet metres away from Vargev's position. A huge explosion engulfed the tower, temporarily blinding the colonel. The few men inside that hadn't been atomised by the heat and power of that particle cannon blast, were engulfed in flames as their uniforms and skin set alight. They ran headlong, screaming in agony and jumping from the tower in a desperate bid to escape the inferno, their bodies slammed into the wet ground far below with a sickening muted thud, the driving rain slowly extinguishing the flames from their broken and lifeless bodies.

The Krenaran force on the landing pad turned their attention towards the large steel doors barring their progress to the loading area. What they had been constructing throughout the day suddenly became all too clear when it unleashed its fury. Like a smaller, portable particle cannon, the force of the shot blasted a gaping hole right through the heavy gauge steel of the door. Three more times the huge cannon roared its anger, and on the third attempt, the doors crumpled and weakened as they were from the depredations of this awesome weapon, were finally blasted apart in a deafening roar that echoed throughout the entire loading area.

The two Dominator assault walkers which Vargev had stationed there, opened fire immediately, a flurry of .50 calibre high velocity rounds from their heavy assault cannons tore into the charging Krenarans with frightening ease. Spent ammunition cases clattered to the ground all around the twin behemoths. The commandoes which had took up positions amongst the parked vehicles behind the dominators also opened fire, the immense hail of assault cannon fire and the commandoes own armschlagers was deafening, echoing all around the vast loading area, still despite the incredible amount of firepower being levelled at them the Krenarans still came on.

The miniature particle cannon opened fire again, smashing into one of the Dominators, its heavy armour no defence against the sheer force of the weapon. A pall of thick smoke spewed from the great rent in the armour of the machine, and it staggered a couple of steps backwards, then burst into flames before finally falling backward with a deafening 'clang' as its steel armour slammed onto the concrete floor.

The lone surviving Dominator desperately tried to continue the defence sweeping its heavy assault cannon in wide arcs, the muzzle flash blinding as dozens upon dozens of heavy caliber slugs burst from its myriad of spinning barrels, more spent casings skittered along the floor.

There must have been fifty Krenaran corpses piled up all along the corridor to the landing pad, nobody had the time to count, just to shoot. Bodies lay everywhere, the stench of charred meat and blood hung in the air, the alien's milky white blood formed into tiny rivulets running down the long ramped corridor to where the freighters were docked above.

The huge Krenaran strode forward on his mechanical legs, giving off a hiss of released pressure as the bird-like feet slammed down on the concrete with such a force that it cracked underfoot. Calmly levelling the triple barrels of his weapon at the equally large assault walker tearing chunks out of his men, he clicked the internal trigger, and, with an intense blast of incandescent green energy, the second Dominator stopped motionless, its weapon hung limply by its side and it appeared to gently stoop forward.

A ragged hole the size of a watermelon had torn straight through the bullet proof cockpit glass, and reduced the pilot inside into crimson jelly that smeared every panel and instrument throughout the interior cockpit. Commandoes defending the loading area continued to rake the onrushing Krenarans with weapons fire, a deafening explosion from a grenade thrown through the breach filled the corridor with smoke, around twenty more Krenarans had fell, the floor turned slippery from their blood.

The advancing Krenarans returned fire and several commandoes were blasted back across the giant warehouse-like room. Landing in a bloodied heap with a crack as their heads snapped back and smashed into the smooth concrete flooring. The surviving commandoes knew they were fighting a desperate battle, and that the loading area was lost, but they had made the Krenarans pay dearly for capturing it.

High above the base, stealth ships continued their attack runs. Several more torpedoes slammed hard into a weakened section of the perimeter wall, sending debris and shrapnel flying in all directions, this last attack was finally too much and a small section of the wall collapsed into a large pile of dust and concrete rubble, the Krenarans had finally succeeded in opening a gap big enough for them to get through.

A lone Dominator advanced toward this gap, the muted 'thump' 'thump' of its feet could be heard as it stomped its way through the muddy grassland, groundwater pooled in the muddy depressions of its footsteps. A single Krenaran managed to scrabble through the pile of shattered concrete and was greeted by a hail of high power assault cannon shells from the approaching Dominator, its body was ripped apart from the impacts of the heavy weapons fire and flung back through the breach.

Their objective complete, the stealth ships turned their attention to the forces defending the main gate, the hastily constructed barricades were already taking a beating from Krenaran weapons fire, the final remaining barricade was torn asunder by simultaneous blasts from two particle cannons, vaporising several soldiers using it as cover. However the firepower from four Dominators, together with cannon blasts from the Apollo battle tanks in support proved too much for the Krenarans, scores of the brutal aliens fell from the barrage of heavy assault cannon fire and the Apollo's high velocity shells, their bodies littering the sodden ground. Those few surviving Krenarans fell back from the main gate, many of which were injured.

The lone, brave Dominator defending the breach in the perimeter wall was relentlessly pouring fire into the oncoming Krenarans, his weapon smoking hot from the friction produced by the rapidly spinning barrels and the hail of hot lead he was pumping into the advancing aliens. Shot after shot raked them as they threw everything they had at the breach, his ammo counter was beginning to run low.

In an effort to help the lone Dominator, struggling against near impossible odds, Vargev ordered some commandoes on a nearby roof to open fire. The awesome firepower unleashed from the commando fire teams' Armschlagers tore into the advancing Krenarans, dozens fell as masses of high power rounds ripped through their alien bodies, their metallic battle armour no defence against solid slugs. Just for a moment it seemed as though the Krenaran were wavering under the intense firefight.

Resolutely however, the aliens returned fire, pressing their numerical superiority. Fire from several of the Krenaran cannons slammed into the walker, knocking it backwards a pace or two, its feet dug a shallow trench in the ground which quickly filled with rainwater as the assault walker weathered the storm of fire. The pilot's cockpit glass was cracked in several places; a large hole was blasted into it just above the pilots head. Its frontal armour was also torn and bent in several areas, exposing the delicate electronics and wiring underneath. The pilot gnashed his teeth, and held fast.

Two of Vargev's commandoes fell, as the Krenarans returned fire on them, their bodies plummeting from the roof of the warehouse. Vargev took aim with his own Armschlager and pressed the trigger, it bucked under the recoil of the high power rounds. One of the brutes fell, clutching its ruined face, a couple of others next to him hugged the wet ground, fearful of befalling the same fate.

The surviving commandoes on the loading platform were not faring quite as well though, embroiled in a desperate rearguard action now as the Krenarans pressed their attack, gaining ground all the time. Three more men died, gaping holes blown through their chests. The massive Krenaran commander levelled his weapon and fired, the resulting blast flung two more commandoes like rag dolls high into the air, their bloodied bodies slamming into the steel clad wall behind them.

The commandoes had put up an intense fight, but the Krenarans were now amongst them, and no human could match an eight foot tall Krenaran for brute strength, almost a dozen commandoes died as the bone crunching impacts of Krenaran fists and kicks snapped necks and broke legs and arms. The few surviving commandoes retreated out of the loading area completely, some were blasted face first into the concrete floor, as Krenarans shot them in the back as they ran, barely five commandoes had made it out alive, and two of them were badly injured.

Vargev, having made his way to one of the warehouse roofs to get a better view had witnessed the retreat; he knew they had lost the loading platform. His commandoes were cut off from the rest of the base as the Krenarans now controlled all of the spaceport and adjoining loading platform, and would very soon occupy the ruins of the command building as well, silently he prayed for a miracle.

The Gamma sun began to crest the distant Valcasian mountains, hailing the beginning of dawn for the third day and the fighting gradually ceased in its intensity, although the occasional crump of pulse rifle fire could be heard as well as the pounding of Apollo shells into the nearby Krenaran lines, who were now busily consolidating on the advances they had made throughout the night. The 'Hell's angels' began counting the cost.

Two Apollo's and a Dominator had been lost defending the main gate, another two Dominators at the loading platform, as well as more than fifty soldiers, both 'Hell's angels' and commandoes were amongst the dead.

Worst of all, General Steel was in critical condition from shrapnel injuries sustained during the defence of that main gate, which meant that Vargev, being next in the chain of command, was now in command of the defence, however, along with his fellow commandoes he was cut off from the rest of the base.

Pacing across the roof of the warehouse, the Russian considered his options which he had to admit, were very few.

Eventually he spied an abandoned Raider A.T.V, partly concealed by the corner of a nearby warehouse. Behind it a 7 tonne truck was parked which the engineers normally used to transport ammunition to the warehouses.

Climbing down from the roof of the warehouse via an access ladder, he motioned for the surviving commandoes to do the same. As they all silently made their way over to him in the cover of the rear of the warehouses, he spoke to the assembled group.

"Listen comrades, we are going to abandon the warehouses and form up with the rest of the armoured company on the other side of the base. But since the Krenarans hold the spaceport and what's left of the command building, we're on our own. To get to the other side, we'll have to use those," he pointed toward the abandoned vehicles.

"Sir, what if we are fired upon, the truck is unarmed."

"We'll cover you from the raider since it has an Armschlager on the roof."

"Understood, sir."

"Okay men, let's move out!"

They made their way towards the vehicles, carrying their injured with them, keeping in cover until they came to a wide road that ran between the warehouse buildings; this was the main route that ran all the way through the facility. Those that could, sprinted across the cracked asphalt and formed into a fire-team on the other side, covering the slower injured men with quick bursts of weapons fire. Eventually they all made it safely across the open expanse of road.

Once there, Vargev quietly signalled that three were to ride in the A.T.V, and the rest in the truck. He joined the others in the Raider, taking the drivers seat. One of the commandoes quickly manned the roof mounted Armschlager, while the other trained his weapon through one of the vehicles fire-ports. The engines in both vehicles simultaneously thrummed into life, and together they both sped off.

The damaged Dominator which had defended the breach in the perimeter wall so bravely, was finally relieved by two undamaged units, strengthening the defence in that area. The lone damaged Dominator slowly trudged its weary way back towards the tank factories for repairs. The Krenarans in the centre largely ignored it they were too busy fortifying their position, besides they didn't think one damaged walker with barely any ammunition left was much of a threat.

Vargev continued to drive down the main road, the Raider rocked gently as the thick all terrain tyres hit the occasional crack and divot in the tarmac, this road connected the warehouse buildings in the east through to the tank factories in the west. And from the warehouses to the munitions factories, where most of the 'Hell's angels' were camped, just over a kilometre away.

The biggest problem lay in getting past the spaceport, loading area, and command building currently held by the Krenarans, as all three were located perilously close to the road. There was however, a large field on the other side of the road, which was used for recreation and some small store houses further ahead. The heavy rain throughout the night had made the ground sodden, so any truck trying to cross that field would get quickly bogged down, Vargev silently cursed his luck.

There was no other choice, they would have to keep to the road and risk the Krenarans opening fire on them. They would have to drive as fast as they could manage, he hoped they would not attract too much attention.

The small convoy closed upon the spaceport, the commando gunner in Vargev's Raider readied the roof mounted Armschlager. The other passenger also readied his weapon. The injured had all been loaded inside the truck since that was the safest place for them, some of the other commandoes were tending to them on route, however their condition was worsening, they needed to get to the triage centre and quickly.

Since the raider was the lead vehicle, Vargev gently pressed the brakes; and steered the raider alongside the larger truck, taking up a position between the buildings on the right hand side of the road and the vulnerable truck where at least the Raider could give the truck some covering fire.

Flashes of bright green energy began to slam into the ground around them from Krenaran weapons fire on the landing pad. The commando on the roof spun around and the Armschlager returned fire, peppering the sides of the tall building. Spent casings clattered upon the cabin floor of the A.T.V.

The truck increased speed, as did the Raider to match. All along the landing pad enemy fire came hurtling towards them, blasting apart thick chunks of tarmac, a shot slammed into the passenger door, blowing a wide hole in it and shattering the bullet-proof Perspex glass, just missing the commandoes leg. Vargev kept going, there was no choice; he had to.

5. The arrival

The Liberty and the remainder of the giant battlegroup was only minutes away from Gamma IV now. The repairs on-route had gone well, however the damage on deck 6 still concerned Michael. The viewscreen shimmered into existence once again, "this is Admiral Sato of the Hermes; prepare to drop out of plasma drive on my order."

The viewscreen gently phased out of existence once again, leaving only the bridge wall.

"Send the acknowledgement," Michael replied.

"Done sir," Kinraid said.

A tense pause fell across the bridge, "here we go, into the lion's den," Michael whispered.

Kinraid looked over at him, "aye sir, nothing the Irish like best than a good old scrap."

Michael chuckled, Kinraid had that innate ability to lighten almost any situation. The viewscreen blazed into life for a second time, "Sato to the fleet, drop out of plasma drive."

"Okay let's do it, drop out of plasma drive, ready all weapons and defensive systems, all hands battlestations!" Michael announced.

At once the command team jumped into life, Eldathar brought the ship out of plasma drive. Logan Jones brought the weapon systems online and charged the exterior hull plating. Across the entire fleet other ships were doing exactly the same, all 188 ships dropped out of plasma drive simultaneously in a gigantic burst of bright white light that was visible for several hundred thousand kilometres.

And found absolutely no trace of any Krenaran activity whatsoever.

"I want full scans every few minutes, sensors to maximum," Michael barked out his orders, where the hell are they, his brow creased in thought.

"Aye cap'n, if they're out there, we'll find 'em," Kinraid said.

"No doubt you will commander," Michael replied, confident in his most senior subordinate's abilities, Kinraid was like a bloodhound with the sensors.

The viewscreen blazed into life once again, "Hermes to the fleet, advance toward the shipyards."

"You heard the man, ahead one half sub-light speed."

Eldathar gently pushed forwards on the arms of the chair, and the Liberty quickly picked up speed.

"Anything yet?" Michael asked, casting a glance toward Kinraid.

"Nothing yet cap'n, wherever they are, they're well hidden."

"Keep trying."

Michael stared intently at the viewscreen as the fleet slowly, cautiously advanced toward the vast shipyards which made up the orbital part of Echo base. Tense minutes passed as the shipyards grew larger as they closed with it, like an enormous flattened orb, docking bays for all manner of ships encircled the main structure, massive communications and sensor towers extended from the centre of the facility like tiny metallic strings reaching up into the infinite vastness of space, the docking bays were all empty however. This was damned peculiar, he thought. The Echo base shipyards are one of the busiest in E.O.C.A space, there were always ships here, either being constructed, undergoing upgrades, or being decommissioned. He knew those Krenaran ships had to be out there somewhere, but where, and how many?'

"What about the shipyards, any life signs on board?"

Kinraid performed a separate sensor sweep of the shipyard interior; studying the findings closely. The light from the console lit up his stubbled features in the darkened command centre.

"Negative sir, no lifesigns," he finally said.

"What about damage to the station itself, anything?"

"None, cap'n; if the Krenarans did take it, they took it intact."

'Nearly two thousand men lived and worked on the shipyards alone, where did they all go?' Michael thought as he rested his chin in his hands, deep in thought.

"I don't like this captain, smells like a trap." Lieutenant Jones said nervously.

"Hold ya' station, Lieutenant."Kinraid said, fixing Logan with a stare.

The Lieutenant nodded his understanding.

Michael said nothing, as he returned his attention to the viewscreen, he knew full well the rest of the crew were anxious. Hell, *he* was anxious. It probably was a Krenaran trap, but right now he couldn't do a damn about it.

"Anything yet commander?" he repeated.

"Nay Cap'n, seems the Krenarans won't come out an' play," Kinraid said as he gazed intently into the sensor systems monitor.

Michael couldn't help but raise a smile at Kinraid's choice of words. Damn, where the hell were they? You don't capture a key shipyard like this, kill everyone on board, and then just abandon it, it didn't add up and he didn't like it for a second. There were too many unknowns here, what happened to the workers on the shipyards? Where were the ships they were working on? And where the hell were the Krenarans? These were three basic questions and Michael didn't know the answers. He hated going into the unknown, because usually it was the unknown that bit you on the ass.

The shipyards themselves loomed large in the shimmering holographic viewscreen now as they neared the facility. The enormous docking facilities were in full view, outstretched servicing pylons and huge repair bays which made the one hundred and forty meter long Liberty look like a tiny speck in comparison.

The lights within the facility were all on, as they could see the thousands of lit viewports, so the base had power. As he gazed into the viewscreen, stroking his chin in thought. Michael noticed that there was not a single scratch anywhere on the station, so they hadn't been in a fight the Krenarans had surprised them.

"Any ships in those docking ports?" he asked just to be sure, their may have been others around the other side of the facility, unseen.

"Negative Cap'n, docking ports are all clear, so they are." Kinraid replied.

Normally there were around twenty ships assigned to defend Echo base, it was all that could be spared from the front lines, and they were ordered to defend the facility at all costs. Where were they? Michael thought.

Suddenly the viewscreen blazed into life again, startling him and breaking him out of his train of thought. "Admiral Sato to the Honduras, and Eurinades, attempt docking procedures. All other vessels, adopt defensive posture." The transmission ended.

"You heard the man, bring us about and adopt defensive position bearing 147 elevation 0," Michael said.

Eldathar instantly complied, and he swung the Liberty 90 degrees, accelerating slightly away from the station and then held position.

Michael looked towards Kinraid who could guess what the captain was thinking, "Still nothing, sir."

The massive Danitza's took up strategic positions around the base, as the Alexander class medium cruiser Honduras, and the Jefferson class heavy destroyer Eurinades advanced toward the station and gradually adopted docking positions.

A formation of Ghandhi class destroyers and Mandela class light cruisers continuously patrolled the area. Other than this the entire fleet sat perfectly still, every ships sensors were constantly screening the surrounding space, as if expecting some sudden strike by the enemy.

On the surface of the planet far below Colonel Nikolai Vargev revved the engine of the raider hard, continuing to speed past the enemy held positions. Energy pulses from Krenaran weapons fire continued to blast apart the ground all around them. The roof mounted Armschlager bucked and swayed as it returned fire; raking the Krenaran positions.

Two of the brutal aliens fell, one gurgling as a shot passed through its neck in a spray of white blood, it plummeted to the ground from the high landing pad. The second was thrown backwards as multiple rounds slammed into its chest. Both the driver of the truck and Vargev in the raider floored the accelerator as they sped past the loading area, and the highest concentration of Krenarans. Yet more energy blasts hurtled towards them and Vargev had to steer hard to avoid the incoming fusillade, smoke and dust thrown up by the weapons fire hammering into the ground all around them. The other commando and the gunner were jostled severely, cursing as he almost lost his grip on the armschlager.

A single lucky shot tore into the roof mounted heavy machine gun, cooking the gunpowder carried within the ammunition and causing it to explode in a bright fireball, showering the occupants in hot metal debris fragments. Vargev very nearly lost control of the vehicle as the force of the explosion rocked the raider violently, causing the A.T.V to veer onto two wheels.

"Not now!" He shouted in desperation, as he wrenched at the steering, beads of sweat lined his chiselled features as he struggled to get the vehicle back under control. The occupants were thrown around the interior of the speeding vehicle, as it jerked violently.

The gunner fell back hard on the steel floor of the vehicle, choking and coughing up blood as he tried to breathe through his ruined airway, his face was a torn and bloodied mess, a burnt ruin from the explosion and shrapnel. Once the A.T.V had settled again the other commando onboard tried to tend to his fallen comrade as the vehicle sped through the hail of Krenaran weapons fire, Vargev cast a quick glance in the rear view mirror, and saw the other commando solemnly shake his head. Silently he cursed.

They quickly passed the fiery ruins of the command centre, fortunately only drawing minimal fire from other Krenarans advancing through the shattered building. They seemed as though they were more interested in consolidating their position for the big push during the night.

Finally the battered raider and the accompanying truck screeched loudly to a halt in front of the huge munitions buildings, Vargev and his accompanying commandoes from both vehicles quickly dismounted, carrying their injured with them.

A young sergeant approached them, and saluted the colonel.

"Where is General Steel sergeant?" Vargev asked as he returned the salute.

"In sickbay sir, he's badly injured. We didn't think you would make it either after being cut off like that."

"We almost didn't sergeant; take me to see General Steel."

"Of course sir."

Vargev followed in the sergeants wake, the colonel felt a slight heat in his right leg, as he looked down he could see that his fatigues and a small portion of his flesh had been singed from the Krenaran weapons fire, while he was driving he had not felt it, ignoring the burning sensation he followed the sergeant inside the temporary triage centre hastily rigged up in a far corner of number 2 tank factory, as far away from the fighting as they could manage.

The factory roof had a large ragged hole blasted into it, as a result of the two days of intensive bombardment. The sunny, cloudless sky of Gamma IV was visible through it, and it leaked water heavily. Conditions were less than ideal, but it was the best they had under the circumstances.

The sergeant and two other medics led Nikolai to a bed where Steel lay.

The general tried in vain to struggle into a sitting position, agonizing pain racked his body however and he collapsed back onto the bed; he was weakening.

"Don't try to move," Vargev said solemnly.

His Generals uniform, hung next to his bed was torn and bloodstained, his exposed chest covered in crimson bandages. "You were right colonel," he coughed.

"About what sir?"

"About everything; about deploying the forces in the hills, I've been a fool and now I've doomed us all." He sunk further into his pillow, a small tear of sadness ran down his weather beaten, wrinkled cheek.

"Try not to speak."

"I guess this means you're in charge now Nikolai." Steel coughed, a small trickle of blood escaped his parched cracked lips.

"Yes sir, it does."

"Just do one thing for me colonel?"

"What's that sir?"

"Win this damned war."

"I'll try my best sir," Vargev smiled wanly, his dark moustache curling up at the corners as he did so.

Walking slowly away from the bed, and out of earshot of Steel, he spoke to one of the medics. "How's he doing?"

"Not good, he has sustained severe shrapnel injuries to his chest and stomach, he has a collapsed lung, a ruptured spleen, and he's bleeding internally."

The medic solemnly shook her head as she let out a sigh, "we are doing everything we can for him, but I don't think he'll last the night."

"Do whatever you can for him."

"We'll keep on trying colonel."

Vargev and the woman saluted each other and he left sickbay, all Nikolai could think about was the fact that there goes a good man, and he will be sorely missed. He couldn't allow himself time to grieve, there will be plenty of time for that later.

He walked towards a group of soldiers smoking and leaning upon the pitted track armour of an Apollo main battle tank. He was weary, and in a daze with the sadness he felt at the loss of General Steel.

A young Lieutenant quickly dropped his cigarette after realizing who it was, saluted and asked. "What are our orders sir?"

"err..what?" Vargev shook his head slightly as if to lift the fog from his mind, before his thoughts snapped back to the task at hand. "We are going to re-organise the entire defence, I want your section to deploy heavy machine gun nests at the front gate, two men per nest; got that."

"Yes sir," the lieutenant snapped to attention. "Is it true what the men say sir?"

"And what is that lieutenant?"

"That we may not last the night out sir," he said weakly.

"We can; and we will Lieutenant. We'll fight to the last man if necessary," Vargev replied, not really believing his own words.

"Yes sir," the lieutenant replied, a slightly relieved look spread across his young features.

They both saluted for the last time and the lieutenant immediately set about ordering his section.

Nikolai could hear the distant 'boom' of entrenched groundhog artillery pieces resuming their day-long shelling of the Krenaran positions.

Sandbags were quickly stacked up near the front gate throughout the day, with heavy machine guns placed behind them. More sandbags were piled up near the breach in the perimeter fence near the warehouses. Vargev had ordered two Dominator assault walkers, and two more heavy machine gun nests there, manpower was on the short side, with so many dead and injured, the men were tired and battle weary, he knew that. But they had to carry on the fight, they couldn't just give up yet.

Troops were ferried past the Krenaran held buildings in much heavier cougar armoured personnel carriers held in reserve, rather than use the lighter raiders. The buildings surrounding the Krenaran occupied areas were garrisoned once again and more heavy machine gun emplacements were prepared at strategic positions on the rooftops.

Finally, after many hours of re-organising and planning, Vargev finally said to himself, "now we are prepared."

In orbit far above, the mood was tense, the Honduras and the Eurinades had docked with the station, and had transferred some of their crew onboard. They were performing a thorough search of the facility, trying to find out what had happened, they found some evidence of weapons fire, but little else, and were about to detach from the station to resume their previous positions.

"Sir, I've got something for ya'," Kinraid said in alarm as he turned in his seat towards Michael. His station came alive with information, data flashed across it with such speed that it was all he could do to read it.

"Put it on the viewer."

The holographic viewer blazed into life again, and they could just about see a small black cloud emerging from the far equator of Gamma IV, silhouetted by the jade green upper atmosphere of the planet itself.

"Magnify."

The viewer zoomed in on the cloud, and they quickly found that it was not a cloud, but instead a gigantic Krenaran fleet heading straight towards them. It showed hundreds of enemy stealth ships, and several of the deadly command carriers bringing up the rear.

"Jesus Christ!" Michael shouted, as he looked upon the size of the enemy fleet bearing down upon them.

"I'm readin' over three hundred ships, and six command carriers," Kinraid said, his eyes wide.

"Have the rest of the fleet detected them?"

"Only the Solarian ships sir, they are awaiting orders."

"The enemy fleet has increased speed, they are closing fast," Eldathar said.

That is how they had taken the station, a fleet of that size would have breezed through the defenders. The crew onboard the shipyards would have been outgunned and quickly overwhelmed, they would have had no choice but to surrender, and in so doing becoming more slaves for the Krenaran war machine, either that or simply eaten, Michael thought sadly.

6. The great battle for Echo base.

The enemy Krenaran fleet continued to close at a tremendous pace.

Michael had now realized that it was all just a monumental trap, the Krenarans knew full well the E.D.F would be sending reinforcements, so they laid in wait on the far side of the planet where they would not be detected. The E.D.F fleet was outnumbered almost two to one, and no less than six of the deadly command carriers were now bearing down upon them.

The Hermes had put its entire fighter and bomber wings on alert status.

The Liberty was already on full alert, its fusion cannon and high energy torpedo launchers, were powered and ready. More power was shunted to the thrusters and main engine. The load on the Solarian power core was almost at maximum, he would have to be careful.

The Krenaran fleet continued its inexorable advance, and Michael noticed that the deadly multiple torpedo launchers on the massive Krenaran command carriers were steadily rising into their firing positions.

As the two gargantuan fleets closed, the signal for battle came from the Hermes. "E.D.F fleet, break and attack!"

At once the two forces set upon one another furiously. Dozens of Solarian battlecruisers, together with their smaller frigates and escorts opened fire together. Multiple incandescent blue fusion cannon beams streaked towards the Krenaran ships, some managed to evade the ferocious fusillade. Several more were caught and torn apart by the sheer power of the Solarian weapon systems, their hulls spinning wildly out of control.

A huge wave of torpedoes launched simultaneously by the Solarian shipping followed this initial strike, slamming into more Krenaran ships at close range, their high power charges smashing into the hulls of the enemy vessels before detonating in huge explosions, lighting up the space around them.

Over twenty Krenaran vessels had been decimated in the initial attack alone, their crumpled, wrecked hulls floating aimlessly through the battle site. Nearby Krenaran ships had to jink and weave to evade the wreckage in order to get to grips with their hated enemy.

On any other day humanity and their Solarian allies would have celebrated the devastation being wrought upon their enemies, however this was not any other day, and was but the tiniest of scratches compared to the sheer numbers of Krenaran ships that fell upon them.

Stealth ships returned fire with their deadly particle beams, targeting the larger, clumsy, and more importantly un-shielded E.D.F ships. The beams smashed home into the hulls of the vessels, causing devastating breaches and massive fiery rents and gouges in the armoured hulls of the vessels.

Several unfortunate Solarian vessels were caught in the withering hail of fire, the green haze of their energy shields lit up, but even these defences could not withstand the onslaught forever, several blinked and died under the barrage, their shield generators simply overloaded.

The Liberty banked around the scorched, blackened hulls of several damaged E.D.F and Solarian ships, its turning thrusters bathing the other ship's hulls in a bright electric blue hue. Two high energy torpedoes from its twin upper launchers caught and blasted apart a stealth ship it was chasing, the explosion wreathed the outside of the Liberty in flame as it then dived low under the gargantuan hull of a Danitza class battleship; its huge starboard mounted rail-cannons thundering above as the small vessel passed by.

The Liberty unleashed the fury of its own fusion cannon. The shot slammed into another stealth ship about to fire on the huge battleship it had just flown past, sending it spiraling out of control by the sheer force of the impact and straight into the path of another, the two craft collided spectacularly sending out a bright fireball that lit up the hulls of the ships all fighting nearby.

One of the enormous Krenaran command carriers launched its deadly salvo of H.O.T rockets, three Solarian ships were utterly decimated by the multiple impacts of the torpedoes, their bright silver crescent shaped hulls torn, smashed and bleeding fire. Everywhere now ships were trading enormous firepower with one another, splintered, devastated vessels floated lifelessly through the void of space.

Towards the rear of the fleet, the E.D.F flagship, the giant Jupiter class assault carrier Hermes was nestled. Its two newly upgraded long range laser batteries picking off Krenaran ships that came too close, however these were not its main weapons, it was a gigantic carrier and its launch doors three and four gradually opened as an entire wing of Peregrine fighters and another wing of God-hammer bombers took flight. Their mission was to eliminate one of those deadly command carriers, thereby making things easier for the fleet to concentrate on the other carriers and ships.

The fighters were to escort the bombers to the target, forming a shield against any Krenaran fire they would attract.

The majority of the Krenaran fleet ignored the smaller bombers and fighters however, instead concentrating their fire on the bigger supposedly deadlier capital ships.

This small formation of twenty four craft flew past the comparatively enormous wreckage of several enemy stealth ships and E.D.F vessels, their hulls torn and shredded, flames licked out of large ragged breaches.

To the tiny fighters and bombers it looked as though they had stumbled upon a clash between feuding titans.

Larger ships flew past and around the fighters as they closed on their target, trading fire with nearby Krenaran vessels. Some Stealth ships would take an occasional pot shot at the escorting fighters, blasting a few of them apart in small fireballs. The shrill death screams of the pilots could be heard over the communications they shared with their wingmen.

As the giant flat topped enemy carrier came into view, they readied their weapons. Those gigantic H.O.T rocket launchers were larger than the fighters themselves, its vast shape loomed before them, dominating everything around it. The small force was down to just six fighters and eight bombers, barely above half strength, but the target was now in sight. And they were resolved to complete their mission; no matter the cost.

The formation increased speed, jinking past yet more devastated shipping, and floating debris fragments. At last they closed with the enemy carrier, it looked as though it was reloading its launchers after expending a salvo earlier in the battle.

The enemy carrier realized its peril too late, as the remaining Peregrine fighters dived upon the colossal ship at full speed, their wingtip mounted short range laser cannon shots raking the deck of the huge vessel. The puny weapon fire barely cut through the thick armour of the Krenaran ship, two of the fighters couldn't break out of their dive fast enough and slammed headlong into the ship, crashing through its hull and sending fires blazing out into space.

As the carrier reeled, the remaining god-hammer bombers seized their chance. Each launched their deadly cobra anti-ship missiles at the Krenaran vessels command super-structure, multiple warheads surged towards their target, their specially modified shape slammed through its thick outer hull armour and then detonated in terrifically bright explosions, sending huge gouts of flame blossoming across the entire command centre of the enemy carrier.

The few surviving fighters and bombers veered away and re-formed ready for the return journey back to the Hermes. Behind them the devastation caused by the missile strike was plain to see, explosions continued to burst apart the command hull of the beleaguered carrier, before the entire structure tore itself apart in a bright fireball, sending a miniature shockwave and debris scattering in all directions, the damage was finally too much for the stricken Krenaran vessel and in an almighty explosion the devastated remains of the ship tore itself apart, a gigantic blinding fireball erupted flinging wreckage in all directions, some of which colliding with nearby ships. A shockwave burst forth which threatened to engulf everything around it as well as the fleeing fighters and bombers.

Two nearby stealth ships were caught by this massive conflagration and they too were torn asunder by the impact of the giant shockwave and their own carrier's huge hull fragments smashing into them.

The Krenarans reeled; one of their prized carriers had been destroyed by the terrans. The entire fleet seemed to hesitate for a few seconds, suddenly unsure of themselves.

The newly upgraded Danitza class battleships Defiant and Vengeance seized upon the brief opportunity and opened fire with their punishing long range high power laser batteries, decimating half a dozen stealth ships unlucky enough to be caught in the withering firestorm.

The Krenarans fought back after their devastating loss, as a multitude of torpedoes smashed into another Danitza, tearing apart its sloped fontal section and ripping its docking arm and delicate plasma drive emitters to pieces. Flames burst out from the multiple breaches, and the massive lumbering battleship looked stricken with the damage it had taken.

The flow of battle ebbed to and fro for what seemed like an eternity to Michael, explosions lit up areas of space everywhere, the ruined and drifting hulls of destroyed vessels now littered the area and were a deadly hazard. Several times Eldathar had to bank the ship sharply to avoid incoming debris or the drifting hull of an E.D.F, Solarian or Krenaran vessel as the casualties mounted on both sides.

The fractured hull of a Jefferson class heavy destroyer listed as the Liberty swooped below it, another Danitza class battleship burned brightly in the distance, its hull pock marked with the blackened craters of torpedo impacts and the deep gouge marks of particle cannon hits.

Two stealth ships shot past just above the Liberty, their speed far too fast for the floating myriad of battlefield detritus all around them, the captured former stealth ship pursued them. The enemy ships weaved to and fro, through the debris of devastated shipping.

"Ready fusion cannon," Michael ordered as the Krenaran ships continued to weave and zigzag their way through the debris field.

"We have target lock," Lieutenant Jones announced.

"Fire!" Michael shouted; fist clenched.

The intensely bright incandescent blue beam lanced out past the destroyed form of an Alexander class medium cruiser, bathing its crumpled hull in a bright electric blue light. The beam tore into the Krenaran ships engines, blasting them apart instantly. The ship careered into a giant piece of hull plating, and then crumpled in a kind of concertina effect before exploding brightly.

The second ship continued to dodge and weave, trying desperately to shake off the far deadlier Liberty, but to no avail, as three high energy torpedoes slammed into the rear of the enemy vessel, it plunged headlong into the blackened ruin of a Washington class heavy cruiser; turning the charred ruin into a flaming inferno once again.

The Liberty continued on its course as up ahead hid the monstrous form of another of the Krenaran command carriers.

Eldathar banked the ship so that it flew between the blackened wrecks of two Jefferson class heavy destroyers which drifted nearby one another. The Liberty levelled out once it had passed the hulks and continued towards its target.

"Is the fusion cannon fully charged?" Michael asked.

"Ninety four percent," Lieutenant Jones replied.

The massive Krenaran carrier recognised the comparatively tiny former Krenaran ship rapidly baring down on its position, its engines were completely different to any typical Krenaran ship, and its weapon systems had been changed, the moment of confusion allowed the Liberty to close with its prey. Recognising the Liberty for what it was, a captured ship, it unleashed three of its deadly H.O.T rockets straight towards it. The deadly accurate missiles raced towards the Liberty with terrifying speed.

"Torpedoes, fire!" Michael shouted in desperation as he saw the bright light of the enemy missile engines streaking towards them. With the little time they had, the Liberty only managed to launch two of its own torpedoes, both the incoming missiles and the ships own torpedoes slammed into one another and exploded in a gigantic, blinding explosion that lit up the space all around them; the shockwave blasting nearby debris in all directions.

Briefly the viewer turned an intensely bright white, Michael and the command crew had to shield their eyes from the blinding light of the explosion.

The Liberty shuddered violently, as the shockwave slammed into it. People were thrown from their consoles; Michael desperately hung onto his seat. As the viewer began to clear, the shape of the third rocket was briefly visible as it hurtled its way towards them.

Completely unable to avoid this third missile in time, the warhead struck home with devastating impact, instantly detonating, and blasting apart one of the high energy torpedo launchers, the sheer force of the explosion sent the Liberty spinning out of control.

Onboard, the scene was one of utter devastation, Eldathar was flung completely from his seat, consoles and sensitive electronics exploded violently; support girders collapsed and fires broke out. Kinraid was thrown into the air and smashed into another console; he lay on the deck unconscious.

The impact was so powerful that the Liberty was flung into a wildly uncontrolled barrel roll. Michael crawled his way over to the navigators chair and tried desperately to regain control of the ship.

The unstable flickering image of the enemy carrier filled the viewscreen as the out of control Liberty sped towards it. Michael heaved on the arms of the pilot's chair with all the might he could muster, if he couldn't steer the ship away from the hull of the enemy carrier in time, they were all dead. His face was grimy as the sweat from the heat mixed with soot from the small fires which had begun to take hold in some parts of the bridge.

He screamed, as he put every last ounce of strength he had into the controls, "come on, you son of a bitch!" he shouted.

The Liberty; barely meters away from slamming into the carrier's deck, responded and Michael had control again. He mashed the button for the fusion cannon, and as the ship made an almost impossibly steep climb, the fusion beam shot out at point blank range tearing a deep fiery ravine down the length of the carrier.

The devastating beam cut a swathe along the centre of the Krenaran ship and up across its command structure, almost shearing it clean in two, it tore itself apart under the force of the cannon impact.

The Liberty had missed careering into the Krenaran ships hull by barely a meter. Nearby Solarian ships, seeing the badly damaged carrier, converged upon it, and mercilessly cut it to pieces with several more fusion cannon hits.

Michael looked upon his debris scattered, smashed bridge, taking in the forms of several mangled E.D.F and Solarian crew members lying motionless on the floor; his heart weighed heavy in his chest as he grieved for them immensely, his head felt fuzzy from the heat and the pain of being thrown around from the torpedo impact.

Since the crew of the Liberty was such a small one, it was like everyone was a friend, and everyone knew everybody else onboard. Michael didn't have the luxury of letting his grief show however, he was in command. And right now they were in desperate trouble, the grief would have to come later.

Logan slowly picked himself up, dusting off his blackened, soot stained uniform. Kinraid slowly regained consciousness and woozily got to his feet as well, his forehead sported a nasty gash from slamming into the console earlier, which bled down the side of his face and onto his uniform.

Michael looked down at the prone form of Eldathar, lying motionless just a few feet from his position at the pilot's chair. Kinraid gradually managed to pick his way through the debris to check over the Solarian, he had been taught basic first aid at the E.D.F officer training centre on Delta base, although he hadn't the faintest idea of Solarian physiology.

He was breathing, but only very shallow, his Solarian officers uniform was torn in several places revealing his blue tinged skin; a viscous blue-ish green blood seeped out of deep cuts and scrapes on the exposed parts of his body.

An emergency damage control team managed to scrabble their way onto the damaged bridge, and began to put out the electrical fires and secured some of the damaged, sparking conduits. The lingering smoke slowly managed to clear as the emergency environmental controls began to take over again, much to Michael's relief.

"What's our status?" He asked rubbing his throbbing head.

Logan made his way over to one of the still functioning internal diagnostic terminals. "Reactive hull armour is down, starboard torpedo launcher is completely destroyed which has left a large breach on decks 2 and 3. We also have some structural damage on deck 4, heavy casualties have been reported; we're lucky it's not worse sir."

Michael pressed his wrist comm. "Alexander to sickbay, we have wounded on the bridge."

"Received, we have a medic team on its way to you now," the familiar voice of Ensign Kathryn Jacobs, the chief medical officer onboard replied.

The small, rather limited sickbay was littered with the wounded, dead and dying. She had been working frenetically to help those most in need. Her long dark locks were bedraggled and knotted, sweat trickled down her gentle youthful features, her bloodstained uniform testament to her work. She quickly tended to a man who had been working in engineering when a backup conduit supplying ionic energy to the starboard turning thruster ruptured and exploded next to where he was standing. His body had received eighty percent burns and most likely would not survive, despite her best efforts.

Passing a hand held E.E.G machine over the body, Kathryn read the readout. It was not good, heart rate was dropping and breathing was getting shallower. She gave the man some adrenaline, to bring his heart rate back up, and his breathing slowly returned to normal.

She had no choice but to use the as yet experimental dermal regeneration booth, or risk losing him again. Asking an orderly to help her with the man's stretcher so she could lay him down inside the booth, which closely resembled that of an old earth C.A.T scanner. She removed his clothes, so that he was now completely naked, which was required for the regeneration effect.

A large scanner passed slowly over the injured man's body and took detailed readings of where the burns were located and how severe. Then another oval shaped device made a pass, barely millimetres from the body itself, coating it with thousands of microscopic stem cells, once this device had made its sweep, a third larger device made a slow pass across the body repeatedly firing very low power electrical impulses at these stem cells. Slowly they began to take on the form of new skin cells; literally growing new skin over the burnt, damaged tissue. The man would need to stay in the booth for several hours yet to encourage the stem cells to grow.

Two medical interns, Crewmen Booth and Mason arrived on the bridge, other than Jacobs they were some of the most experienced medical staff on the ship. Although the medical staff was only five strong fully manned, the other three were inundated in sickbay.

They shook their heads when they came upon the unconscious form of Eldathar, pulled out a foldout stretcher they were carrying, and carried him off to sickbay. A quiet sadness welled up inside Michael as the Solarian was carried away, Eldathar was far and away the best pilot he had, and one of the best in the fleet, his cheery personality was infectious and he dearly hoped he would recover, he considered the Solarian one of his closest friends. A few minutes later the medic team returned, checked over the other bodies and finally turned to Kinraid's head wound.

Mason placed a synth flesh bandage on it and said, "you should be fine now commander."

"Thanks."

"Ensign Hawkins to the bridge," Michael spoke into the internal comm.

Several minutes later, Ensign Jeffrey Hawkins arrived on the bridge, he was the relief pilot onboard, and took the place of the injured Eldathar. Michael had nothing against the guy, but he didn't really trust him, probably due to the fact that he was absolutely green, a raw recruit, straight out of the pilot training centre on Delta alpha base. And in these circumstances you could do with an experienced pilot you could trust to fly you out of a tight spot. He just hoped Mr. Hawkins was up to the task.

"We've got another problem cap'n," Kinraid announced turning back to his flickering screen.

Why is nothing ever easy anymore, Michael thought with a depressed sigh.

Kinraid brought it up on the viewer, the shape of two stealth ships were rapidly closing down on their position. The Liberty had managed to drift away from the main battle. The bright streaks of weapons fire and flashes of explosions were still clearly visible in the distance.

"Head for the planet," Michael commanded, he prayed the damaged Liberty would hold together through the entry into the atmosphere of Gamma IV.

"Sir......the Hermes," Kinraid said as he looked at the viewer, it zoomed in to depict the massive carrier.

The gigantic wedge shaped ship was ablaze, multiple torpedo impacts had smashed into its superstructure, and it was listing badly. Giant Explosions erupted, bursting apart sections of its elongated triangular hull in great gouts of flame.

"There's nothing we can do for her now," Michael said sadly.

The pursuing stealth ships continued to close on the Liberty.

7. Liberty down.

Nikolai Vargev was busily putting the finishing touches to his newly reformed defences. Dusk was beginning to set in, and he knew the Krenarans would resume their attacks soon.

The engineers were already busily repairing the multitude of vehicles damaged over the course of the fighting. Everyone was blissfully unaware however of the huge battle still raging high above the planet.

There were a couple of things Vargev needed to attend to before the inevitable attacks resumed. Heading over to one of the temporary repair bays the engineers had rigged up in one of the vast tank factories. Nikolai wanted to meet the man who piloted that dominator which defended the breach so bravely the night before. He asked one of the guards, who pointed to one of the assault walkers which was awaiting repairs at the far end of the repair bay.

Two engineers were busily welding together some of the frontal armour plating damaged in the attacks. Its cracked cockpit glass had been replaced with one from another unsalvageable dominator.

Standing next to the battered walker, overseeing the repairs with his back towards Nikolai, a lone man was stood. Vargev made his way over to the man who was a little startled by the colonel's presence.

Quickly turning on his heel, he saluted, which Vargev dutifully returned. The man was only young, perhaps in his early twenties and possessing of a thick mane of dark brown hair.

"Are you the man who piloted that dominator defending the breach last night?" He said pointing towards the mammoth war machine.

"Yes sir, Corporal Greystoke, sir."

"That was some fight you put up last night corporal, how long have you piloted dominators?"

"Five years sir, me and Bertha go everywhere."

"Bertha?"

"The name of my dominator, big Bertha," Greystoke motioned for Vargev to follow where he revealed an airbrushed picture of a voluptuous woman in a tight red dress and holding a machine gun in one hand. Underneath the image, it read Bertha in scarlet italic. The corporal had carefully painted the image on the rear power supply cowling.

Vargev smiled, "quite an artist too corporal."

Greystoke silently nodded, patting the exterior of the machine. "Don't worry Bertha, we'll get you patched up in no time."

"I'm going to see to it that you're promoted to sergeant, Greystoke, when we finally get out of here."

"If I may sir, I would rather prefer to stay at the rank I am sir."

"Why?"

"If I remain corporal, I simply go where I'm sent and fight where I'm needed, there is no command decision to make sir."

"I see," Vargev replied, eyeing the young corporal, concerned about the young man's lack of aspiration. "You don't want to be in command, to lead men out into the field?"

"No sir, I am quite happy being the man at the bottom, without all the rigours of command sir."

"You know corporal, you're a wiser man and a better soldier than most of my senior Lieutenants."

"Thank you sir," Greystoke replied with a warm smile.

The two men saluted once more, and Vargev went to leave, but at the last minute he turned back, "corporal."

"Yes sir?"

"I want you to assist in the defence of the main gate, as soon as Bertha is ready."

"Yes sir," Greystoke nodded respectfully.

They saluted once more and Vargev left the building.

Now he angrily strode over to one of the vast munitions factories, and picked up an Armschlager heavy machine gun from the armoury inside the factory, he had business with someone. He asked the quartermaster of the armoury, "Where's Kalidis?"

"Last I heard he was up in number 3 tank factory sir."

"Thanks," Vargev replied as he left the building; figures, the furthest tank factory away from the fighting.

He hefted the heavy Armschlager with one hand as he strode out of the munitions factory towards number 3 tank factory, the sling dragged slightly on the ground. The second equally important task had come upon the colonel.

He walked slowly and purposefully towards the tank factory, Kalidis was an engineer and not a soldier, however he was still an E.D.F general and in command of the facility, if not the defenders. And while Nikolai's men were giving their last breath to defend it, Kalidis was hiding out in a factory saving his own ass. The general's cowardice infuriated Vargev, and if he could not convince him, the Russian was not above putting a bullet in the general; court martial be damned.

Inside the building it was dark, the power supply must have been cut to this area. He slowly looked around, allowing his senses time to adjust to the gloom.

Nikolai listened intently for any sign of movement, for the slightest inkling of Kalidis's presence. There was nothing, carefully Vargev made his way further into the factory, continuing to look around him and taking in his surroundings.

He quietly made his way up a series of aluminium steps, in order to get a better view of the interior, and continued along a long gantry which ran the length of the factory, giving access to a series of four overhead cranes which lowered the heavy turrets onto the partially built Apollo hulls lined up below.

Vargev continued to make his way along this gantry, careful that his footsteps did not give away the colonel's position. The metal grating he walked across creaked slightly, still no sign of Kalidis, I bet the fucking coward's ran off, he thought, pursing his lips in anger.

From behind him he heard the faint, almost imperceptible shuffling of feet.

"You're getting old Vargev, a commando colonel surprised like that is not good," Kalidis scoffed.

He was holding a single shot laser pistol directly behind Vargev's head. Nikolai could just about feel the cold steel of the barrel resting against the back of his skull.

"Drop the gun!"

Vargev had no choice but to comply, and the Armschlager fell onto the gantry with a loud metallic clatter.

"You know, you really are underestimating me Kalidis," Vargev said calmly.

"I don't think so, not this time, especially since I'm the one with the pistol trained on your head."

Kalidis's voice was thick with venom, he hated Vargev, hated the fact that he was this perfect commando; built for war, and he was little more than a glorified mechanic, Vargev seemed to get all the plaudits; where were his?

"You're underestimating me if you think you surprised me."

Kalidis blinked, and in a blur Vargev spun around and simultaneously swiped the weapon out of his hand. It sailed through the air and over the gantry railing, skittering off one of the tank hulls below.

Without even leaving the general a chance to react, Vargev cuffed Kalidis across the mouth, sending the commander of Echo base sprawling onto his backside and rattling the gantry. Blood streamed from his cut lip.

"I'll have you up on charges for that, you bastard!" he snarled as he wiped the blood from his mouth.

"For what?" Vargev replied, "a piece of shrapnel flew off the tank factory wall in the firefight. Besides I wonder what charges you'll face," he said as he casually walked over to the struggling general.

"The head of Echo base letting the entire facility fall to the enemy, and like the coward you are, not lifting a finger to prevent it. Pretty unbecoming of an E.D.F senior officer don't you think?" Vargev retorted, he was ice cool and wasn't playing around, Kalidis was a coward and he hated cowards especially those of the higher ranks, and he had no problem shooting Kalidis for it if he was pushed.

Kalidis slowly stumbled to his feet as Vargev approached, swinging a vicious right hook towards the Russian's chin. The blow was slow and clumsy, the colonel easily caught his fist and smashed his elbow into Kalidis's nose, the general staggered backwards; his shattered nose pumping blood down his mouth and chin.

Kalidis turned and made to run back down the gantry, desperately trying to escape. He realized that he was grossly outmatched. Vargev was the faster however, and the Russian charged after him, their heavy boots making the gantry shudder as they ran.

Nikolai quickly caught up with the general and rugby tackled him to the ground, the entire gantry rattled violently under the force of the two men slamming onto it. Kalidis attempted a wild kick at Vargev's head, but completely missed the colonel. Nikolai then crawled over the prone form of Kalidis, using his powerful muscles to hold the cowardly general still as he clasped his hand over the general's throat.

Breathing slightly heavier, he lowered his face close to the Kalidis's, his eyes bored into him and he bellowed. "Listen to me, you little prick!" the colonel's voice boomed as it echoed around the deserted tank factory. "To me, you're nothing but a fucking coward! And I would kill you right now, but I need every man I can get, even a snivelling little waste of space like you." He squeezed a little tighter as if to emphasise his point, Kalidis coughed and gasped for breath as he writhed in a desperate bid to escape Vargev's clutches.

"What would you have me do!" he spluttered, "I'm an engineer, not a fucking soldier! I fix vehicles, not fight wars."

"Well tonight, you're both." Vargev replied sternly, not letting go just yet. "I want you to lead your engineers as you would any other day. I want you to work them like they have never been worked before, repairing the vehicles that are helping to save your sorry ass."

"Okay okay, I will," Kalidis spluttered again.

"You had better do; because if you don't, all that will be left of you once I'm finished is another casualty statistic.........comrade." Vargev finally released his vice like grip on Kalidis, he scrabbled unsteadily to his feet.

"Yes, fucking sir." The general coughed, his throat was raw from the near strangulation he received from Nikolai.

"That's better."

Retrieving the heavy Armschlager, he pointed it in Kalidis's direction. "Now get out of here, you have vehicles to fix."

Slowly the general made his way down the gantry, clutching his still bleeding nose. Vargev watched him leave and clicked on the safety switch on the side of the weapon.

"And Kalidis!" he shouted down from the top of the gantry.

The general turned to look back up at Vargev.

"At the first hint of trouble I hear from you." He pressed the trigger on the weapon, and a loud click reverberated around the factory. The echo made it sound even more ominous.

Kalidis simply grunted and trudged away.

One of the worst things Vargev despised was a coward, and Kalidis was one, but Vargev had no other choice, he didn't have to like it though.

Nightfall was now rapidly descending, and he made his way quickly to the front line. Offering a small prayer to the motherland far away, he silently begged for his men to hold for just one more night. In reality, he probably knew it was his last, for three nights straight they had fought intense, bitter firefights. His men were tired and low on ammunition.

Vargev couldn't see any way of holding the base, they were simply outgunned and damn near overrun. He checked his webbing, only two clips left for his weapon, he would have to make every shot count. Taking up position with the rest of the commandoes who he had ordered to defend the main gate, he surveyed the blasted, scorch marked fields beyond. Already he could pick out movement, this is where the fighting would be fiercest, he and his men would fight like dogs, fight to the last man drew breath than see a single Krenaran step through those gates.

The Krenarans began to resume their attack. Artillery pieces thundered as they resumed shelling the advancing alien's positions, loud explosions blasted earth and Krenaran alike high into the air. High velocity shells from strategically placed Apollo battle tanks pounded into the advancing aliens.

Despite scores dying, still more of them came on through the onslaught. Those that couldn't walk or had lost limbs, crawled through the muddied, blasted ground toward their hated enemies, not giving up for an instant.

Vargev waited until they got into range, before bellowing out the order. "Open fire!"

The roar of multiple Armschlagers all firing in unison, together with the heavy machine gun nests was deafening and awesome in its fury. Tracer fire lit up the main gate as a storm of rounds punched into the Krenaran positions. Big Bertha, and the other dominators added their awesome firepower to the mix, its heavy assault cannon glowed red hot as it poured fire into the Krenarans, cutting great swathes through them, over fifty had fell, their armoured reptilian bodies littering the fields.

Where those had fallen, yet more took their place, heedless of the horrific losses they were taking, the Krenarans still inexorably advanced.

The huge weapon the Krenarans used to breach the loading area doors was now trained on the Dominator's defending the breach in the perimeter.

The miniature particle cannon buzzed and crackled with barely contained power. Before the Dominators could even react, the operator unleashed the full fury of the weapon, the incandescent green energy beam shot forth once again. One of the machines was hit in the rear, the force of the weapon tore its power plant apart in a deafening explosion that showered the entire area in razor sharp shrapnel. Its flaming wreckage was thrown forward due to the force of the impact and smashed through the perimeter breach.

The second Dominator turned to engage this new threat, however the particle cannon opened fire again. Against a weapon of such power the walker had no chance, its leg was blasted clean off; the war machine toppled backwards onto the perimeter wall itself. A third shot decimated it in a bright ball of flame, lighting up the broken concrete wall and the nearby breach in a bright fiery glow.

The huge Krenaran commander, Alax, stood on the landing pad and oversaw the destruction the weapon had caused with a satisfied grin, the weakling E.D.F have failed, Echo base is ours, he smirked evilly at the thought.

Vargev, embroiled in a titanic fire-fight at the main gate had suddenly realised something was missing. Where were the stealth ships that had been pounding them on previous nights?

For some unknown reason, he ventured to look behind him. There in the night sky he could just see a tiny faint shape moving towards them. His heart sank, here come the fucking stealth ships; right on cue.

As the enemy ship approached, he noticed that this one was badly damaged, it was partially on fire and trailed smoke. Then Vargev noticed the blue indented thrusters on either side of the ship, and realised it wasn't an enemy ship at all.

"It's the Liberty," he thought aloud.

Two stealth ships were pursuing it, Vargev could plainly see bright flashes of weapons fire in the night sky, as two particle cannon shots slammed into the rear of the former captured stealth ship, it was losing altitude quickly.

With an almighty crash, it slammed into the field at the rear of the base, throwing up huge plumes of earth and gouging a deep trench into the ground as it hurtled uncontrollably towards the base. Its underside screeched over the road sending out a shower of sparks, and the whole ship smashed into the main loading area, slowly coming to rest partway inside the huge structure itself.

Vargev knew that he was hard pressed at the gate, as the firefight intensified, several commandoes lay dead on the tarmac, huge holes blasted through various bloodied body parts.

However he had to make sure that the people onboard the Liberty were okay.

"Grenades!" He roared over the din of battle, as a cannon shot blasted into the tarmac next to his foot.

Together, the surviving commandoes each took out a single grenade, pulled the pin, and as one, hurled them into the Krenaran lines. A thunderous ripple of deafening explosions tore through the enemy, showering the commandoes in dirt and Krenaran body parts.

That should make them keep their heads down for a bit, he thought as he grabbed the five nearest commandoes and made his way towards the Krenaran controlled loading area.

Big bertha covered them as they made their escape, Greystoke winked down at them as he piloted it. The twelve foot tall war machine stomped its way up the road to reinforce the gate, spraying the advancing Krenarans with heavy assault cannon fire.

Vargev, together with the five other commandoes headed towards one of the munitions factories and climbed aboard an unmanned raider A.T.V, one of them instinctively manned the ubiquitous heavy machine gun in the roof. Luckily the keys were still in the ignition, Vargev started it up and the engine quickly thrummed into life. With a spray of mud from the heavy tyres the vehicle accelerated back towards the main gate.

He chose a slightly more difficult route towards the loading area, between the perimeter fence and the Krenaran occupied buildings, as it would attract less weapons fire. However this was almost all off-road. Nearing the main gate itself, the occupants saw that the fighting had reached its peak, scores of Krenaran and human bodies lay on the road, crawling, shouting, and screaming. The constant chatter of weapons fire was everywhere and the stench of smoke hung thick in the air.

The commando manning the roof mounted Armschlager, swivelled the weapon and opened fire as the vehicle sped along the road. The heavy machine gun bucked and swayed as large calibre rounds thumped into the enemy, the unmistakable sound of empty bullet cases clattering onto the floor of the vehicle once again greeted Nikolai.

The big Russian commando steered the raider off the road, and set off east into a small expanse of field separating the ruined command building from the perimeter fence.

Those Krenarans that had taken up positions amongst the ruins began opening fire on the raider, blasts from their weapons thumped into the ground all around the vehicle

The Armschlager opened fire again in return, blasting apart thick chunks of masonry as the commando gunner sprayed the Krenaran positions with lead. The other four began returning fire through fire ports in the high tensile polycarbonate windows. Two Krenarans screamed as they were hit, tumbling into the dirt.

Vargev yanked the steering wheel hard, the raider skidded and turned south throwing up great clods of earth and grass as it sped between the ruins and the loading area. However, they were now attracting weapons fire from both buildings.

A shot smashed into the passenger side of the A.T.V, and the commando sitting next to Vargev suddenly went limp. His weapon clattered onto the foot-well of the 4x4.

The other commandoes opened fire through the fire ports once again, several Krenarans fell from the buildings as shots slammed home, landing with a dull, wet thud on the ground below. The roof mounted Armschlager raked them with yet more fire.

Nikolai sharply turned the vehicle east again, and skidded through the mangled front façade of the loading area.

The Liberty dwarfed them, jutting out of the front of the building where it had come to rest. Sparks from flailing circuits fizzed and popped around them, smashed girders and crumpled metal debris littered the floor from the colossal impact of the 149 metre long ship crashing headlong into the structure.

Four Krenarans were cautiously advancing on the stricken ship, the roof mounted Armschlager quickly silenced them in a deafening hail of rounds. They fell to the floor gurgling, white blood oozing out onto the smooth concrete floor.

Vargev quickly grabbed his weapon and climbed out of the vehicle. He did a quick visual scan of the Liberty, it had sustained heavy damage, its rear engines were a mess and one of its torpedo launchers reduced to nothing more than twisted scorched metal. He had never seen the Liberty take such a beating. Jesus, he thought, this thing looks like it's been in world war three.

He ordered the rest of the commandoes to cover the position as he attempted to enter the Liberty by opening the port crew hatch. With a weak hiss of de-pressurised air, the hatch opened and the colonel clambered inside.

The interior did indeed look like a scene from world war three, main power was down and the lights were out. Vargev fished out a small torch from a pouch in his webbing, and fixed it to the barrel of his weapon.

Shattered displays threw out sparks from damaged conduits, smashed girders and various detritus covered the floor, the colonel had to pick his way through carefully.

Crewmen were slumped on the floor in various places, some dead and some merely unconscious.

He continued carefully picking his way through the ship, his torchlight throwing up shadows in the gloom. Some sections still had power, probably running on emergency backup. How long it would last, he had no idea. It was nearly eight months since Nikolai had last set foot on this ship and it felt, strangely enough, as if he was getting re-acquainted with an old friend.

He managed to make it to one of the main elevators, which, luck would have it, were still operable.

"Bridge," he said as he stepped inside, a garbled acknowledgement came through the speakers before slowly taking him to his destination, although noticeably slower than he remembered.

The bridge doors would not open, and with a heave, he managed to open them just enough to crawl through. The stench of smoke and melted circuits was present throughout the whole ship, but especially so here, it hung thick in the air, and his throat felt raw, he hacked and coughed occasionally, Nikolai saw that many of her crew were laid motionless on the floor.

One man groaned as he shuffled uncertainly, trying to get to his feet. He had a deep ragged gash on his upper arm which had stained his royal blue uniform a crimson colour. In addition to another wound on his forehead, just above his right eye.

Vargev quickly made his way over to the man in an effort to help, and as he neared, recognised the man as his old friend Michael Alexander. He held out a hand to steady him.

"What the hell happened comrade?"

Michael held up a hand to his forehead, it throbbed painfully, "we were in a huge battle in orbit, we were hit, one of those damn command carriers. Drifted for a while before we regained control, then chased by two stealth ships before we crashed." He lapsed back into unconsciousness.

Vargev gently shook the weakened Michael to awaken him again, "stay with me," he said studying his friend. "Did they bring any reinforcements?"

Michael slowly opened his eyes again, "no, we came in a fleet, over one hundred and eighty ships, and the biggest fleet we ever put together. However, the Krenarans, they had three hundred. We were outnumbered almost two to one. The battle is still being fought in orbit.

Michael lapsed into unconsciousness a second time, however a medic had managed to make it onto the bridge, looking somewhat battered himself, his white uniform was blackened and torn in several places.

"Over here!" Vargev called out in the darkness.

The medic made his way over to them, and studied Michael intently before bandaging his wounds with synth-flesh patches. "He's in shock, and he has lost a lot of blood."

The medic laid Michael flat out on the floor, and put together a portable stretcher. "I need to get him to sickbay; will you help me carry him?"

"Of course," Vargev nodded.

They carried the unconscious Michael down to sickbay, where Kathryn Jacobs, the British chief medical officer, gave him blood. Gradually Michael came around, he recovered quickly.

"wha....where are we?" he asked.

"In sickbay," Vargev reminded him.

"No; where are we?"

"On the surface of Gamma IV," Nikolai replied.

"Good, so we made it through the atmosphere then?"

"Yes, you made it through the atmosphere, although your landing sucked."

"Err...yeah, sorry about that. It's good to see you again Nikolai, it's been a while."

"It's good to see you too, old friend."

Michael looked up at the gentle form of Kathryn tending to him, "Well I suppose it had to happen some time."

"What had to?" Kathryn replied.

"You had to save me, since I rescued you on Delta base all those months ago."

Kathryn silently smiled as she continued to tend to his wounds.

Michael was soon on his feet however, and with no small amount of arguing from Miss Jacobs, left sickbay.

The lights gradually came back on, indicating that all the backup generators had now kicked in, Nikolai unclipped his torch from his weapon and placed it back in his webbing.

Kinraid joined them, and greeted Vargev. "Hello there colonel," he saluted, "Heard a lot about ya', so I have."

"No doubt you have," Vargev replied, saluting in kind. He was unsure about Kinraid, although he was reluctant to make any judgements about the man. He had never met him before.

"How's the ship?" Michael asked the commander as the three of them walked together.

"She's taken quite a pasting cap'n, we don't know if she'll fly again."

"She will," Michael smiled confidently, "it will take more than a little crash landing to keep her down, she's a tough little cookie," he paused as he rubbed his temples, his head still throbbed, he was still feeling the effects of concussion from the crash. "Any news from the fleet in orbit?"

"None sir, communications are still down."

"Damn, okay I want a full damage assessment in one hour commander; get to it."

"Aye sir," Kinraid said as he left the two men alone.

"He seems like a good man," Vargev said as they continued along the debris-strewn corridor.

"Yeah, he is one hell of an officer too," Michael replied with a nod.

8. The defeat of Alax

The chatter of machine gun fire could be heard ever so faintly just outside of the ship, and then all went silent once again.

"The other commandoes!" Vargev cried as he realised, he sprinted back towards the hatch.

"I'll come with you," Michael replied as he chased after him.

Together they ran the length of the corridor to the elevator that would take them to deck 6, the lowest deck on the ship, and where the hatch was located. Soon enough the elevator deposited them, as the doors opened they sprinted down the main corridor on the deck, making a sharp right turn, about half way along, and located the hatch.

Vargev slowly crept out, keeping his body close to the hull of the downed ship. The distant echo of explosions and weapons fire was still audible from outside the loading area. The commandoes and the rest of the armoured company were putting up one hell of a fight, Vargev thought. It made him proud.

He looked around the immediate area as Michael clambered out of the hatch behind him. The raider was still intact, however along the interior of the loading bay lay the bullet-ridden bodies of a dozen or so Krenarans, freshly culled.

The commando manning the roof mounted Armschlager was dead. His head was a mangled, bloodied ruin. The other commandoes were also dead, laid amongst the Krenaran bodies.

Vargev made his way cautiously over to one of the commando bodies, picked up its weapon and ammunition, and tossed it over to Michael.

Silently, the big Russian pointed to the wide ramped corridor that led up onto the spaceport platform. Together they sprinted across the loading area to the edge of this corridor. Vargev peered around it, half expecting a dozen more to come at them.

Instead, there was nothing, no sign of movement, just dead silence. Carefully the two of them made their way up the gentle incline, and were almost halfway there when they came upon the gigantic form of the Krenaran Vargev spotted earlier. Oh, this is not going to end well, he thought.

Close up, it looked even more terrifying. Dwarfing even Axus, whom they killed eight months ago, and he had been no pushover, in fact, he had damn near killed them both.

Its heavy mechanical legs hissed and crackled with power. With heavy footfalls that pounded the very ground, this behemoth of a Krenaran slowly, ominously advanced towards them. Its huge triple barrelled cannon levelled straight at them.

This monster regarded them as though they were nothing more than little inconveniences, to be crushed by his merest whim, "I am Alax, overlord of the Krenaran race, and you had better pray to whatever deities you believe in, because only they can help you now!" The aliens voice boomed across the length of the corridor.

The sight of this massive lumbering Krenaran triggered something in Michael's mind, suddenly he went back to that time eight months ago, trying to remember something important, damn it, he couldn't remember what it was.

Reality rapidly snapped him out of his reverie when three simultaneous beams shot forth from Alax's weapon, they both dived in opposite directions as the shot flashed past them and blasted a sizable crater out of the concrete floor.

They both let loose with their Armschlagers, the roar of weapons fire was deafening around the deserted corridor; the weapons juddered as round after round pumped into the oncoming leviathan, spent cases tinkled and danced off the hard floor. A transparent yellow haze formed around this lumbering beast of a Krenaran, and the shots simply ricocheted off it.

"He's got some sort of god-damn energy field!" Michael shouted in desperation.

"No shit! Like I didn't know that!" Vargev retorted.

Another blast shot past the Russian and they retreated, stumbling down the corridor and back into the wider loading area.

Slowly, inexorably, as though death itself; Alax followed after them.

"We have to get to the raider, it's our only chance!" Vargev shouted.

They ran further into the loading area, with Alax in pursuit. The only advantage they had was that for all his power, all his brute force. Alax was slow on those mechanical legs of his, although it wasn't much of an advantage.

"Now I remember!" Michael said, as his mind returned to that time eight months ago.

"Remember what!" Vargev shouted over the increasingly loud footfalls behind them.

"Eight months ago, when we fought Axus," Michael said breathing hard."

"Yeah, what about it?" Vargev replied as they raced towards the safety of the parked raider.

"Axus said that he had a master, and he was going to deliver us to him."

"And this guy must be it."

They almost made it to the raider when three blindingly bright green energy beams shot past them and smashed into the vehicle. Vargev and Michael both dived out of the way as the sheer force of the impact smashed the 4x4 onto its side, its engine caught fire and began churning out thick black smoke.

"I have wasted enough time with you pitiful humans, prepare to die!" Alax said, with such an evil uncaring tone to his voice, these Terrans were nothing to him, weak insects to squash at his merest whim.

Both Michael and Vargev were down, as the force of the blast had momentarily dazed them. Their heads were swimming as those heavy, pounding footfalls continued to close, there was a kind of grim finality to those ominous footfalls, maybe this was one enemy they couldn't defeat or escape from.

Together, both of them picked up their weapons and opened fire at the hulking great Krenaran in one last valiant attempt to bring it down, its yellow energy field blazed into life once again.

It was at that point that Vargev accepted his fate, this enemy was simply too powerful, too strong, they were hopelessly outmatched and deep down he knew it; there was just nothing he could do against an enemy of such power.

The battle at the main gate had intensified, the constant chatter of heavy machine gun fire and intermittent buzzing of pulse rifle shots, met the powerful 'wuu-doom' of Krenaran energy weapons. Both humans and Krenarans were dying in equal measure in the bitter fighting.

The wreckage of a blazing apollo main battle tank, and a dominator assault walker was spread out across the road. Surviving commandoes and infantrymen were using it as a kind of makeshift barricade.

The Krenarans were continuing to press the attack, throwing everything they had against this gate despite the horrific casualties the E.D.F troops were inflicting on them.

A shot from a Krenaran weapon blasted apart the head of a heavy machine gunner, the crimson spray of blood and brain matter coated the nearby sandbags in a deep red sheen. A dozen Krenarans tried to charge the sandbagged position, but were mercilessly ripped apart as the heavy assault cannon of big Bertha roared its anger.

In the loading area, the battle was every bit as intense, as Michael and Vargev raced past the huge Krenaran, trying to use their speed to their advantage, their lungs burned, patches of sweat, blood and grime marked their skin.

The enormous trunk like fist of Alax tried to swat them as they sprinted past, but only whipped through fresh air.

Michael spied a covered metal box at the top of one of Alax's mechanical legs, a small light blinked at the top of it. Michael had an idea what this was.

"Aim for the shield generator at the top of its leg!" he shouted to Vargev, pointing to this box.

Alax opened fire with his weapon again, the Russian barely had time to jump out of the way of the blast as it narrowly missed turning him into crimson froth. The shot blew a large hole in the metal clad wall behind with a loud explosion.

He hit the ground hard; face first, his weapon skittered away across the floor. The thunderous footsteps came closer. Vargev, now winded was breathing hard desperately searching for some kind of weapon, anything he could use.

"Move! Get out of there!" a desperate Michael shouted over to him.

It was too late; Alax had him. With one enormous hand hefted Vargev high into the air, and held him close to the aliens face, the colonel could feel his hot breath on his face, as those evil crimson eyes bored into his own, "you have troubled me enough, and now I will crush you like the bug you are." Then flung him like a rag doll into the corrugated steel wall behind. The Russians body smashed against the hard cladding with such force his body went limp.

"Bastard!" a desperate Michael shouted, as he let rip with his weapon. Blood and sweat trickled down the Liberty captains face.

A returned shot from Alax's weapon made him dive for cover to his left as the shot barely missed him. He hid amongst the burning wreckage of the raider.

"Face it Terran, you cannot defeat me, surrender and I'll end this quickly."

Michael was fast running out of options, there had to be something, anything he could use against this thing.

Then he spotted it; the damaged dominator. Its cockpit glass was shattered and the pilot was dead, but it looked reasonably operable. It was the only thing even capable of hurting this monstrosity.

The thump, thump of heavy footfalls were slowly getting nearer, he needed a distraction.

Vargev gradually came to, and quietly got back woozily to his feet, he was in agony, his ribs felt busted, he blinked as his vision slowly cleared and looked over to Michael, Alax was almost on top of him and he was keeping cover amongst the wreckage of the raider. He noticed he was pointing towards something, as though trying to tell him something, Nikolai looked to where he was pointing; the damaged dominator, and instantly knew what Michael was thinking.

"Keep him busy," he whispered hoping Michael could read his lips.

"Easy for you to say," the reply came.

Michael continued to play cat and mouse amongst the burning raider, Alax was slow and easily evaded. He was desperately tired though and wondered just how long he could keep it going.

Vargev removed the bloodied remains of the pilot from the dominator and strapped himself in, wiping the gore from the instruments. The machine was in fairly good condition, a status panel was showing damage to the frontal armour plates, and that the glass was indeed shattered making it open to the elements. Nevertheless, other than that it was okay. The weapons and hydraulic systems worked fine anyway.

He had never piloted a dominator in action before, and had only trained on one a handful of times. Slotting his arms into the weapon mounts, and his legs into the leg mounts. As he moved the machine accentuated his movements via the hydraulics. He managed to get the thing to roll onto its front so it could right itself, no mean feat considering this thing weighed nearly four tonnes.

With a noticeable whine, the machine managed to get back onto its legs again. Alax immediately turned towards this new threat.

"Hey asshole, time to pick on someone your own size!" Vargev shouted through the smashed glass with an evil grin.

He clicked a trigger with his left hand, and the assault cannon unleashed a hail of rounds into the Krenaran, its energy field glowed brightly as it deflected the furious salvo, bullet holes riddled the roof and walls from the deflected rounds. The rapidly spinning barrels of the dominator's assault cannon glowed red hot as Vargev pumped round after round in a hailstorm of bullets. The status display flashed a warning at him as it registered a danger of overheat on the weapon, Alax staggered backwards under the fusillade, digging in his metal claws on the hard concrete.

One of the bullets must have found its mark as the Krenarans shield generator crackled and sparked, its energy field shut down. However Vargevs weapon had overheated and jammed, damn it, he thought.

Alax looked at him and smiled an evil smile, calmly levelled his own weapon and fired. The shot tore into the assault cannon, blasting it apart in a hail of razor sharp shrapnel. The machine staggered backwards, and almost toppled over. Nikolai screamed in pain as his left hand burned, barely managing to keep the thing from falling.

He moved his legs, coaxing the machine into a clumsy parody of a jog. The dominator bore down on the equally huge Alax, the massive machine and the Krenaran overlord slammed into each other, rolling end over end, grappling and wrestling with one another.

Alax tried to shove his weapon through the cockpit glass in an effort to blast Vargev apart at point blank range, however with the hydraulic ram attached to the hard point on the other arm, Vargev repeatedly smashed aside the blow.

The Krenaran gripped and tore at the frontal armour, rending steel with his bare hand in a furious effort to get to Vargev, Alax became crazed, frothing at the mouth, his reptilian features contorting in pure fury. He roared his rage.

Ultimately, the dominator unable to withstand the furious assault fell backwards in a deafening crash, the Krenaran heaved itself on top of the machine, pounding down upon it with its fist, blow after blow smashing into it.

Lying face up and being violently thrown about by Alax's assault, Vargev clicked another trigger in his right hand; Alax froze. Where a mere split second ago there was an enormous tussle raging, now there was serene calm.

Vargev had activated the hydraulic ram in the right hand weapon mount, when he pressed that trigger he released four thousand pounds per square inch of pressure, forcing the solid titanium tipped ram forward with such a force that it tore right through the Krenarans body.

The Russian simply laid there, totally exhausted and in extreme pain from his badly burned hand and broken ribs. The dominator torn and mangled from the machinations of Alax, damaged now beyond repair.

Michael hurried over to his position, and gently helped Vargev out of the battered machine, the Russian winced as his broken ribs sent shooting pains across his right side.

"Well I guess we are even now."

"Even, about what?"

"Well, I killed Axus and now you finished off Alax."

"The hell we are." The big Russian coughed.

Michael pushed a button on his wrist comm. "Alexander to Med-bay we need a medic down here pronto."

"Received, we'll get one to you now." The voice of Kathryn replied.

As the two of them waited for the medic to arrive, Vargev spluttered, "listen."

"What for?" Michael replied, his brows furrowed, trying to decipher anything out of the ordinary.

"The weapons fire has stopped," Vargev replied as he favoured his ribs. "The battle must be over."

"Or all your men are dead, and those Krenaran bastards will come marching in here any moment."

There was a faint buzzing sound coming from behind them, Michael looked around trying to locate the source of the strange sound. It slowly increased in its intensity, finally he realised it was coming from the fallen body of Alax. Small arcs of energy were discharging from his body in vivid flashes.

"It's some sort of self destruct, it must have activated when his heart stopped, we've got to get out here now!"

Michael supported the injured Vargev, as they tried to make a break for it, the Russian tried to run, however, whenever he did agonizing pains shot across his mid-section.

Michael pressed his wrist comm. again. "Michael to Liberty, transfer any power you have left to the gravitic engines, and get the hell out of here; fast!"

"Copy, gotcha cap'n," Kinraid replied.

The crippled Liberty slowly began to power up. On the battered bridge, Kinraid asked. "How much power do we actually have?"

"We have ten percent reserve power remaining, nowhere near enough to break orbit, even if we were in any condition." Johnson Logameier, the chief engineer replied.

"Okay, divert whatever power we 'ave left, and set us down on that field we crashed in."

The low pitched whine of the Liberty's gravitic engines grew louder as they thrummed into life, gently the vessel began to rise, a deafening screeching sound rang out as twisted metal rubbed against metal, loose parts of the loading bay it had smashed into began crashing to the ground all around as the Liberty struggled to free itself.

Michael and Nikolai shielded their eyes as they hobbled away outside the badly damaged building. The engines of the comparatively huge Liberty barely a few meters above them were blowing dust and debris in all directions, several razor sharp metal fragments blew perilously close to the escaping men.

Vargev risked a quick glance backwards, he could see a bright blue light through the swirling dust and detritus, energy was arcing and dancing furiously now, it was reaching critical mass.

"We've got to get clear; it's going to blow any second."

As fast as they could manage, the two of them hobbled their way out of the loading bay, pieces of torn metal and roof, dislodged by the retreating Liberty continued to crash down all around them, narrowly missing flattening them both.

The dark, black hulled ship overhead increased her speed as the remaining power was shunted to her gravitic engines. Smashed and bent support girders from the structure came crashing down as the ship forcefully freed itself. Eventually it was clear.

Michael and Vargev had made it barely twenty metres from the structure when the device detonated in a gigantic blue-white blast that sent them both slamming into the ground.

The huge explosion had deafened both of them temporarily, the shockwave reverberated throughout the entire structure, causing the weakened roof to collapse completely, a vast plume of smoke and dust arose from the almighty explosion illuminated by the fires within, before dissipating high in the night sky above them.

The entire base was briefly illuminated by the massive detonation, and many who were busily fighting thought the Liberty destroyed. However, there it stood in the torn ravaged field across from the main thoroughfare. Near to where it had first crash landed, and this time safely nestled atop its landing legs.

9. A truce declared.

Michael and Vargev both struggled to their feet, blackened, bloodied, and in Vargev's case in agony, nevertheless they were still somehow alive. Both had injuries, Michael still hadn't fully recovered from the crash, Vargev's arm and ribs were in a bad way.

Kinraid, Jacobs, and another medic came to their aid. "Jesus, that looks like some fight you two had over there," Kinraid said as Jacobs and the other medic checked them over.

"We need to get both of you to sickbay, straight away." Kathryn said.

After a short pause, Michael asked, "what's the prognosis, doc?"

"You're bleeding internally again, colonel Vargev here has third degree burns to his left hand and upper forearm, as well as multiple fractured ribs."

"We had best do as the good doctor says," Michael said.

"You won't get an argument from me."

The sun was just beginning to rise over the distant Valcasian mountains, the shrill darkness of night was gradually giving way to the pale light of a new morning, and ending what was the worst night of bloodshed of them all.

Barely a fifth of the troops posted to defend the main gate had made it, many were wounded and the battlefield triage centre was swamped. The desperate cries of the dying could be heard as faint wails blown across the wind. The gate itself looked like a scene from hell. The still smouldering wreckage of three apollo battle tanks were strewn across the road at odd angles, casting a pall of thick black smoke over the area. The fallen forms of three dominator assault walkers were also ablaze, adding to the scene of desolation.

The sole remaining dominator to survive the onslaught was 'big Bertha' its assault cannon completely empty of ammunition. It sported several rents and tears in its armour, and its hydraulic ram was slick with the Krenaran blood it had spilled during the night. Its bullet proof cockpit glass was completely shattered, inside stood its pilot, corporal Greystoke, tired, battered, and with a deep ragged gash that seeped blood down the right side of his face. Still, he stood victorious.

Later that day Vargev was released from the med-bay of the Liberty, a few sessions in the dermal regeneration booth had largely healed his horribly burned arm. His ribs were healing gradually, the doctor had injected a drug known as protenase directly into the bone marrow of his ribs, to accelerate normal bone growth. However, they still plagued him and would for at least a week, so Kathryn had advised him.

He was quietly sat on the collapsed form of a concrete column, silently taking in the desolation, hundreds of good men lay dead or dying defending this place, the base was virtually in ruins due to three nights of intense fighting. The constant smell of smoke and death hung in the air, he watched as wounded soldiers piled up the broken bodies of the dead, once proud men reduced to charred, bloodied corpses.

To Vargev, this was the true horror of war, not the fighting, but the aftermath. Counting the cost and feeling everything his men went through, because he was one of them.

With a deep sadness he knew that his men, although they fought valiantly, every last one of them. They were in no position to mount an effective defence for a fourth night, Echo base had fallen and his heart sank.

I will make sure that people will know what had happened here. Those five hundred men held out against a vastly superior Krenaran force for three whole nights and gave every last breath to defend a key supply base against these monstrous Krenarans who would destroy it.

A small tear ran down the grizzled commando colonel's cheek.

A young Lieutenant, by the name of Cole approached him and saluted, Vargev tried to return the salute, however he couldn't, whenever he lifted his arms his ribs felt like they were on fire, the lieutenant understood however.

"Sir, it's the Krenarans, they have stopped their attack and one of them wants to speak with you."

He snorted, so now they want to talk. It's not enough that we've been pummelled into oblivion, now comes the inevitable surrender and you'll all be spared plea; predictable.

"Thank you Lieutenant, tell him I'll be right there."

Michael was still in sickbay and had fallen unconscious again, his condition had worsened. Kathryn monitored him closely, fearing for her captain's life, he couldn't die, he was Michael Alexander, the heroic captain of the Liberty, and one of the most famous and decorated officers in the E.D.F, and she needed him.

Vargev returned to the sickbay of the Liberty to watch over his friend, Kathryn had informed him of Michael's condition and Nikolai spent some time at his friend's side, silently watching him, the damned Krenaran can wait.

Finally, he said softly. "I've got to go now old comrade. I shall see you soon."

With that, Vargev left sickbay and Michael alone while Kathryn carefully monitored him.

He walked with Cole to a raider parked not too far from the damaged Liberty.

"I think you're going to have to drive lieutenant," Vargev smiled weakly as he carefully clambered inside.

"Yes sir," Cole drove the raider as carefully as he could manage across the bumpy grassy field, and back onto the broken tarmac of the road, he then hung a right and drove straight towards the main gate.

A small group of Krenarans had gathered amidst all the wreckage, they were armed, several infantrymen and a couple of commandoes had their weapons trained on them.

Cole parked the raider fifty feet or so further up the road, and they made their way down towards the small group. Looks as though these Krenarans were captured or surrendered, Vargev thought. However he remained silent, wondering how this would play out.

The lieutenant spoke first, "this is the highest ranking officer currently present here; his name is colonel Vargev."

"So this is the legendary Colonel Nikolai Vargev, you have garnered a fierce reputation amongst my people. I am Dalvosh, second in command of Krenaran forces after lord Alax. Your men have fought with honour and bravery, and have earned the respect of the Krenaran people."

"Err....Thank you." Vargev replied, still waiting for them to demand his surrender.

"Let this day mark the end of hostilities between our peoples, both sides have already lost far too much in this needless war," Dalvosh continued, nodding his head almost reverentially at Vargev, who was dumbfounded, could this be the first peaceful Krenaran, or was it just a ploy.

"First, have your men lower their weapons," Vargev said. "Then we'll talk."

"If we do that, your men will kill us," Dalvosh replied.

"My men are trained to obey my orders."

"As are mine."

Both sides readied their weapons; long, tense seconds passed as Vargev eyed Dalvosh who at eight feet tall was considerably shorter and leaner than Alax, but still towered over the colonel nevertheless, who was attempting to discern any trickery in those deep red eyes of his. Dalvosh did likewise, he knew full well that Vargev was a deadly and implacable enemy of the Krenaran people and would not hesitate to kill them all, given the chance. Or that was what he had been taught.

Both commanders almost simultaneously ordered their men to lower their weapons, after a few more tense seconds both groups lowered them. The sense of mistrust between the two commanders was still thick in the air, and they continued to eye each other suspiciously.

"What about the thousands of slaves you took during the war?" Vargev asked, remembering that horrible time at the now ruined Agemman colony.

"As soon as an official ceasefire treaty can be drawn up, your slaves will be returned to you. The Krenaran empire no longer wants this war, it has cost us too much already with the loss of two of our greatest leaders, together with the loss of ships and troops."

"We can draw up an unofficial ceasefire right now, for a permanent treaty to be made official it would have to be signed on Earth in front of the E.O.C.A council, or in the presence of an elected member. However, our communications have been knocked out."

"Then this is what we must do," Dalvosh said.

The remainder of both forces were assembled at the bombed out wreckage strewn remnant of the main gate. Hundreds of men and Krenarans had gathered, although the men were largely outnumbered by the lumbering Krenaran warriors.

Vargev looked up into the clouds of the early morning sky, and let out an audible sigh of relief, the war was finally coming to a close. As he continued to contemplate the sky, he could just make out the contrails of shuttles and transports descending through the clouds towards their position. His sense of relief grew rapidly as the myriad of small craft headed his way; help had finally arrived.

The few commandoes left alive and the troops of the 'Hells angels' all let out a great cheer, throwing their fists into the air as the shuttles landed in the debris strewn fields between the abandoned Krenaran trenches and Echo base itself, the sheer sense of jubilation from those men who had fought so hard to defend this place was palpable.

More troops, E.D.F naval personnel and Solarians disembarked the numerous craft and headed to where Vargev, Dalvosh, and the survivors were gathered.

What appeared to be a high ranking naval officer approached them flanked by a few soldiers of his own.

"Captain Ericsson of the Tempest, I'm assuming we are here to accept the surrender of Krenaran forces in this area?"

Vargev took a long look at this 'captain', who the hell was he to waltz in here like this. Finally he said, "no surrender captain; peace, this Krenaran here." He motioned towards Dalvosh, "is the new leader of the Krenaran military, he wants a ceasefire."

"What about the war still going on across the other colonies?"

At this Dalvosh finally spoke up in his deep, rasping voice, sounding very much like his throat had a bagful of shale tipped down it. "Not just here, everywhere. We no longer want this war, it has cost us too much already," he repeated for the captain's benefit.

"Peace, well I'll be damned, I've forgotten what peace feels like." Ericsson replied with genuine surprise.

Vargev allowed himself a slight chuckle.

"I'd better get back to the Tempest and contact E.D.F command, let them know of the situation, although my ship has taken quite a beating itself."

The captain excused himself and made to leave the men when Vargev stopped him. "If you don't mind me asking captain, how did you get here?"

"It's a long story colonel, I'll fill you in when you get onboard."

Aboard the damaged Liberty, Ensign Kathryn Jacobs was carefully monitoring Michael Alexander, he was still unconscious and his condition was steadily getting worse.

Commander Quinn Kinraid was stood over the captain's bed, watching. "After all tat he's done; all tat he has accomplished. To just give up and die now like this, is just a waste," he whispered to the medical officer.

"He's a fighter; he'll pull through. He has to." A small tear ran down the ensigns gentle features.

He had been haemorrhaging internally and had gone into anaphylactic shock, Jacobs had brought him round, kept him alive somehow. He was losing twelve pints of blood in three minutes, and if Kathryn hadn't operated as early as she did, he would have been dead by now.

The heart monitor continued its slow beeping, the sound thudded into their ears as the two of them silently stood over the frail form of their captain, they waited anxiously. Beep….beep…beep.

"We have done all we can, it's up to him now." She whispered.

"Keep me informed ensign," Kinraid said as he left the small sickbay, although inside the pain he was feeling at watching his captain and friend slowly slipping away like this was tearing him apart, he had to keep some emotional distance, he was in command now, and the crew, albeit severely demoralised was counting on him.

Arriving on what remained of the shattered bridge, he touched a control on his wrist comm. "lieutenant Logameier to the bridge."

Johnson Logameier had his head inside an access hatch of the primary power conduit of the ruined main engine, trying to affect some emergency repairs, when his wrist comm. buzzed; startling him, he bumped his head against a rather hard piece of insulation plating, cursing and rubbing his throbbing head, he answered, "on my way."

A few minutes later and he arrived back on the bridge, walking up to Kinraid he asked, "yes commander?"

"I need an update lieutenant, how are the repairs coming?"

"Slowly sir, she has taken a heck of a beating, power should be restored to the main engine within the hour, although it would be several more hours or even days before we are able to use it. As for the damaged launcher, we are not going to be able to repair that until we reach Delta base, and there has been significant hull damage from the crash."

"Will she be able t' make orbit?"

"In her present condition, no commander; we'll burn up trying."

"Damn," Kinraid replied with an exasperated sigh, "how long?"

"We're looking at weeks, sir."

The flicker of an idea began to form in Kinraid's mind, "wait a bloody minute." He whispered, more to himself than to anyone else. "We need a major base for repairs, right?"

"Yes sir."

"Well, what in the name o' god have we just bloody well crashed into?"

"Commander, the people here are more accustomed to building military vehicles and munitions, not naval systems."

"T'ey are E.D.F engineers, some o' them will have expertise repairing vessels o' the fleet, they have a whoppin' great fleet yard in orbit and transfer men to and fro all the time." Kinraid was becoming more excited, a plan was coming together and he knew it.

"All the shipyard functions are in orbit, and we don't know if the E.D.F fleet was successful or not without communications."

"True, but tat's not to say that it can't be done now is it," Kinraid replied, "I'll get Kalidis, he'll be able to help us, so he will. Lieutenant, you're with me."

Logameier sighed, still unsure as to how this would work, however Kinraid was in command now, and he had no choice but to follow his orders.

The two officers made their way towards the port access hatch and exited the ship, sealing the hatch shut behind them.

Once they stepped out onto the windswept field, they appreciated first hand the sheer scale of the devastation. Ahead of them in the distance, the smashed loading area lay crumpled and smouldering. The once tall command building reduced to nothing more than a pile of rubble.

Soldiers bearing the wounds of bitter fighting milled around performing their duties as best they could.

The two men made their way onto the main road, still littered with debris and the occasional smashed vehicle; medics carried soldiers on stretchers, horrifically wounded and pumped full of morphine and other pain killing drugs.

Kinraid wondered if ever there was a hell, this looked like it.

As they made their way towards the main gate, they were greeted by more scenes of horror, the wreckage of blasted apollo's and dominators lay smouldering across the road. Medics were everywhere trying to cope with the sheer backlog of wounded and dying. Acrid smoke still hung like a pall in the air, accustomed to breathing the recycled, purified and filtered air of the Liberty, it nearly choked the two officers.

Either side of the road, rows upon rows of body bags were laid, each one inscribed with the occupants name, rank and serial number, a grim reminder of the horrible reality of war; people died.

They made their way over to the most senior person they could find, a young sergeant. The two officers saluted the sergeant before Kinraid asked, "Excuse me, do you know te' head o' this facility?"

The sergeant looked at them rather strangely, "I'm rather busy here commander." As he set to the task of bandaging another soldiers wounded forehead.

"Ahem, I'll ask again," Kinraid replied, his tone growing more menacing. "Do you fecking know, who is in charge o' this fecking shit-hole!"

Startled by the sheer force in Kinraids words, the sergeant straightened immediately, and addressed him properly. "Err, yes commander, it's General Kalidis sir, he is overseeing repair operations, number 3 tank factory."

"Thank you, would you know where that is now?" Kinraid replied.

"I'll have someone take you," the sergeant suggested.

He shouted over to an even younger looking man, "private! Take a raider and these two men over to number 3 tank factory."

"Yes sergeant." The private motioned for Kinraid and Logameier to follow him to a nearby unoccupied raider. This one was surprisingly undamaged, quite a rarity.

"If you would like to follow me."

"Diplomacy works every fecking time," Kinraid whispered to Logameier next to him, who quietly smiled.

The three of them climbed into the small transport, the young private who looked barely in his twenties started the engine and the 4x4 sped off towards the tank factory.

"Your part of the Liberty crew aren't you?" The private asked curiously, noting their different uniforms.

"Guilty as charged," Kinraid replied.

"You guy's are like regular Robin Hoods, always popping up out of nowhere and giving the Krenaran's a bloody nose before sodding off again, if you beg my pardon."

"Really?" Kinraid and Logameier looked at one another, genuinely surprised at this. "Well this time it was us who got the bloody nose, otherwise we wouldn't have carved out a four hundred meter trench right through that field over there."

After a few minutes the Raider pulled up in front of number 3 tank factory, with a gentle squeal of its brakes.

The building had taken some light damage during the fighting, a few smashed windows here and there, and the occasional dent and hole in the steel cladded exterior, all-in-all it had emerged remarkably well. Being situated in the far south west corner of the base far away from the main fighting had also helped its cause.

A formidable queue of smashed, torn and blasted vehicles had formed outside however, occasionally a patched up raider or an apollo would rumble its way out towards a parking area at the west side of the building.

As the three men made their way inside, they found that it was a hive of activity. Almost two dozen damaged vehicles were parked up in bays forming two long rows, four engineers to every vehicle. Bright welding arcs flashed continuously, casting deep shadows across the interior and sending sparks splashing across the floor. The buzzing of grinders and cutting equipment sounding like a swarm of angry bees about the place.

A tall, thin man was barking out orders in the centre of the vast tank factory, "Johnson how is the rotator on that turret, Finlay, double check the inlet manifold on that raider. Jackson, that dominator should have been finished half an hour ago, come on people, these machines aren't going to fix themselves!"

Kinraid and Logameier made their way over to this man, the private who was accompanying them said, "I've got to get back to the main gate."

"Yeah, see you kid." Logameier replied.

"Quite some operation, you have going here," Kinraid said to the man.

The man stopped and turned to face them, Kinraid immediately noticed that the bridge of the man's nose was taped, and he sported a hefty black eye. The commander thought nothing of it, most men around here bore some sort of war wound. "Needs to be, nearly thirty damaged vehicles a day are coming through here, the names Kalidis."

He shook both of their hands, suddenly a loud bang reverberated throughout the bay, and one of the raiders let out a cloud of white smoke.

Kalidis spun around to the source of the noise. "Idiots, you didn't check the fuel cells for ruptures!"

"General, we need your help," the two men asked in unison.

"Join the queue, a lot of people need my help right now."

"You don't understand, it's not a vehicle we need help with."

The general looked at them with a hint of disdain. "All I know is your holding up this operation."

"It's a ship," Logameier said.

This got the general's attention, he stroked his chin thoughtfully, "a ship, here?"

"It's the Liberty, she's crashed and we really need her to be able to break orbit." Kinraid replied.

Dalvosh, Vargev, and Captain Ericsson boarded the E.D.F shuttle, its gravitic engines gently whined as they powered up. Gradually the small craft lifted off, and headed towards the upper atmosphere. While in flight, Ericsson told them about the battle above the planet.

"It was the biggest fleet action of the war, one hundred and eighty eight E.D.F and Solarian ships took part, we were led by Admiral Sato of the Hermes. When we arrived in-system we found nothing, not even the Solarian ships could find any trace of Krenaran activity." Ericsson pressed a few controls, levelling out the shuttle as it continued its ascent through the clouds.

"As we moved into docking range of the Echo base shipyards, we picked up the signatures of no less than three hundred and forty one stealth ships, led by six command carriers." Ericsson sighed as he remembered the awful sight of that enormous fleet bearing down upon them.

"To begin with the battle did not go well, they decimated us, we lost over fifty ships in the first few minutes. The Solarian ships acquitted themselves well, when the first of the Krenaran command carriers fell to a bombing run from the Hermes bombers they began to go on the defensive." He said, a smile beginning to form on his lips.

"The Liberty, and a handful of Solarian ships accounted for another. That really put the wind up them, the Krenarans fought back, but now they were panicking and disorganised, they became easy pickings for the Solarian battlecruisers who tore into them, although the Hermes itself never made it." Ericsson paused for breath, smiling at the memory of the destroyed Krenaran ships littering space around his ship. "The remaining Krenaran ships retreated and abandoned the planet. We were in no shape to pursue however, so we re-grouped at the shipyards. With barely fifty ships left, most of which were heavily damaged."

"Jesus," Vargev said in reply, "and I thought you would never come."

The shuttle shuddered slightly as it cut through the high altitude winds before gradually breaking into orbit, leaving the emerald green atmosphere of Gamma IV behind. The stars and faint outline of the shipyards were gradually revealed to them.

As they neared the vast shipyards, Vargev got his first glimpse of the sheer scale of the carnage that had taken place here.

What remained of the E.D.F/Solarian fleet was clustered around the newly re-taken shipyards, in the distance hundreds of damaged, broken hulls that were lost in the fighting floated lifelessly, mere corpses of the proud vessels they once were. It was an enormous graveyard, a testament to the scale of the fighting that had taken place here.

Many of the ships that had survived the battle bore the scars of their ordeal. Where once sophisticated weapon systems had been, there was only twisted blackened metal, with only the occasional spark from shredded power conduits revealing the extent of the damage. Ruined plasma drives trailed bright plumes of energised plasma into space.

Vargev felt a small tinge of guilt at his impatience at questioning whether reinforcements were forthcoming in the battle on the surface. As the shuttle began its approach toward the station, he now saw that things had been just as desperate up here, he had no idea.

"Shuttle tempest one-niner to echo base, requesting permission to dock," Ericsson spoke into his console.

"Confirmed, clearance granted for bay four," came the reply.

The shuttle altered course slightly, veering around one of the gigantic upper docking pylons of the base, before landing in one of the smaller docking areas built into the hull of the station. Once the shuttle had landed, the bay was re-pressurised and a small access ramp descended from the craft.

Vargev stepped out onto the wide, flat hangar bay. He noticed the bay was packed with various other shuttles transferring the wounded and supplies to and fro from vessels still unable to dock with the station. The comparatively enormous Dalvosh then emerged from the shuttle, ducking his reptilian head as he did so, Ericsson was the last to leave the shuttle as he powered down the small craft.

"What's the casualty count?" Vargev asked.

"Don't know; final figures still haven't come through yet." Ericsson answered, "best guess puts it at around forty four thousand dead."

As they made their way through long corridors choked with wounded naval personnel, Vargev couldn't help but feel a sense of pity for what these men had gone through.

Dalvosh simply stomped his way through the jeering crowd, uncaring and unheeding of these men's plight, he knew they hated him, he had been their most hated enemy for the better part of a year, and the feeling was definitely mutual.

After what had seemed like an eternity, they finally arrived at the vast command section of the facility. There, stood in the recessed centre section of a huge circular room were twelve captains all talking amongst themselves. As the three of them entered the room they turned their attention towards them, studying the blackened, weary face of Vargev, then Ericsson, finally they turned to the huge form of Dalvosh and eyed him with a look of pure hatred.

"What is a Krenaran doing on this station captain Ericsson?" They asked pointedly.

Dalvosh spoke up, "I have come to establish peace with our two races in the form of a non-aggression treaty." The words sounded hollow, "though we may never be friends, both of our races have already lost too much in this war, and that is why it must end now."

"Impressive words Krenaran, but why should we trust you?" One of the arrayed captains replied.

"A Krenaran warrior stood in a Terran built station advocating peace should be all the proof that you seek. That, and my master Alax is dead, he was the head of the Krenaran military. Now I must take his place, which grants me the power to speak for my people."

One of the captains then gave a command to a younger naval officer manning a station on the upper periphery of the room. "Open a communications channel, I want a direct channel to alpha base, get me Admiral Mason."

"Yes captain," the officer replied.

After a brief pause, Admiral Mason's wizened features appeared on the viewer of Echo base.

"Yes captains, what is it?"

"Echo base has been secured admiral, and the Krenarans wish to discuss terms to end the war, they want peace in the form of a non-aggression treaty."

Mason's brows furrowed noticeably, "you have proof of this?"

Dalvosh stepped forward towards the viewer, "My name is Dalvosh, I am the new head of the Krenaran military and lord Alax's successor, I am standing on one of your stations in peace, surely this is the proof you seek."

"My god!" The admiral gasped, and promptly paused the communication.

"What is he doing," Dalvosh asked Ericsson, quizzically.

"Probably wondering if he's dreaming," the captain replied.

A long pause passed, before Mason's face re-appeared on the viewer again.

"A small team of E.O.C.A diplomats have been scrambled from Sicarius, they are carrying the official documents for the treaty, it will be five days until they are able to reach you."

"That will be acceptable," Dalvosh nodded.

On the surface, Kinraid, Logameier and Kalidis were busily assessing the damage to the battered Liberty.

Kinraid turned to the general, "do ye' tink ye' can get it into orbit again?"

"Normally I'd say no, but with what's been happening around here lately I'm not so sure. It needs the hull fractures sealing, as well as the destroyed launcher, otherwise it will just burn up as it attempts to get out of the atmosphere. We'll have to rig up a new main engine, we'll need to contact people in orbit for that."

"How long do ye' tink it'll take?" Kinraid asked.

"It should be ready in about a month."

Kinraid gasped. "A month!" then sighed, "understood, I'll organise te' Liberty repair teams to assist ye'."

Over the course of the next week, shuttles went to and fro, ferrying supplies from the echo base shipyards to the planet below. Engineers swarmed over the Liberty, repairing hull fractures and replacing damaged systems. The Solarians lent their aid also, and donated a Solarian Ionic drive system, from one of their own damaged escorts.

Kathryn Jacobs spent most of the week monitoring the weak form of Michael. Towards the end of the week his results showed a marked improvement, her excitement began to increase as she knew the captain was beginning to pull through, finally four days after being rushed to sickbay, Michael awoke and looked visibly stronger.

"What's our status?" He asked weakly.

"Always down to business aren't we, well the repairs are continuing, and the Krenarans are due to sign a peace deal tomorrow which will officially bring an end to the war. It's being broadcast all over E.O.C.A space, there's street parties and massive celebrations being planned all over the outer colonies. Its almost like all of humanity is breathing a giant sigh of relief." Jacobs replied, her smile could barely contain her excitement at the prospect of the war being over.

"How long until we can get back into orbit?"

"Not for another three weeks at least," Kathryn replied as she studied his vital signs monitor for any signs of change.

"So are we just supposed to sit on our hands for three weeks," Michael retorted, growing a little angry at the situation they had found themselves.

"We don't have a choice, besides you're not cleared to leave sickbay yet anyway."

"The hell I'm not!" Michael shouted angrily, sat bolt upright, and made to leave.

"I could order you," Kathryn replied calmly.

Michael thought about this for a moment, before finally conceding and laying back down on the hospital bed, "I guess so, besides the last time I went against your orders, it nearly killed me."

"Well, no one was expecting you to go gallivanting off and fight a huge Krenaran monster straight from your hospital bed, were they?"

"Gotta have something to do during the day," He winked and smiled.

Ensign Kathryn Jacobs simply tutted, "you're unbelievable," before going back to her duties.

The next day Michael was feeling something like his normal self again, and had been cleared to leave sickbay. Kathryn had prescribed him light duties only for the next few weeks, and plenty of rest. Suddenly a one hundred and forty nine metre long ship seemed awfully small when on the surface of a planet. He went to pay Kinraid a visit outside of the ship, partly to escape the confines, and partly to find out what he had missed, finding that Kalidis was with him.

"Glad your up on your old feet again cap'n," Kinraid said with his customary Irish twang.

"Thank you, what's our status report," Michael replied getting straight down to business.

"The engineers have sealed around forty percent of the hull fractures, and the main breach where the launcher was has been sealed. The new Solarian engine is fitted but not powered up yet."

Michael looked upon his ship, its matt black silhouette glinted dully in the light from the morning sun, flashes from welding arcs lit up parts of its dark hull. He and this ship had been through more than their fare share of scrapes together, and he was confident she could get through this one as well.

"This ship is much more than just a ship, it has become a symbol of hope and strength to the E.D.F; it needs to be back in orbit doing what it does best."

"My engineers are working flat-out trying to get it spaceworthy again as soon as possible. We know how important this ship is to the E.D.F," Kalidis replied.

"Good, so what's this peace deal the Krenarans are going to sign anyway?"

"Apparently, te' Krenarans want to sign a non-aggression treaty with E.O.C.A, tey are saying that both sides have already lost too much in this war. An E.O.C.A diplomatic team are arriving in about tree hours time," Kinraid replied.

"Think they'll keep it?" Michael asked with a hint of sarcasm in his voice.

"I'm not really sure to be honest; yeah, the Krenarans were te' ones who started this whole thing in the first place. But te' new head o' the Krenaran military, this Dalvosh, isn't like Axus or Alax, it looks like he just wants to put 'tis whole sorry mess behind him and go home I tink."

Michael laughed, "well I've heard it all now, a Krenaran who's tired of fighting. That's a new one on me." Looking across to the heavily damaged spaceport and half-demolished loading area, he noticed that it was completely clear of Krenarans, they must have cleared out, linked up with the rest of them outside the base, he thought.

"The negotiations are to take place in a temporary headquarters, set up in number 1 tank factory, apparently it is more historically fitting." Kalidis said, rolling his eyes.

Michael harrumphed, "well is it now," a sarcastic tone to his voice. "I hope that history remembers that the vast majority of the atrocities in this war were caused by them, Aurelias and Sigma XI spring to mind." He remembered those horrific attacks during the first days of the war, thousands perished within minutes. Michael reserved a special hatred for these Krenarans, for what they did to mankind, and for the deaths of his wife and son. The war had embittered him, and he didn't think the hatred would ever pass. In fact, he didn't really want it to. He changed to subject to bring him out of his dark thoughts, "anyway, what happened to those Krenarans on the spaceport?"

"Tey retreated as soon as the fighting stopped, and re-joined the main force outside te' gates," Kinraid answered.

Later that day a single Washington class heavy cruiser glided slowly towards the orbital shipyards, the lights from the facility played along its newly upgraded high powered upper laser turrets, and equipped with under-slung torpedo launchers underneath its sloped almost pyramid like frontal section as used by the Ghandhi class destroyers. Considerably smaller than the huge Danitza class battleships, its weapons lacked their range. Up close, the Washington class could unleash a powerful salvo of its own, and those torpedoes made it a dangerous foe for any ship to face, its weaknesses where that it could be picked off rather easily from distance as, being a heavier ship, it lacked the manoeuvrability of the faster Ghandhi class, and could be vulnerable to enemy bombing runs.

Captain Ericsson was temporarily in command of the shipyards, and watched the relatively tiny ship approach through the viewer, when the face of a young and rather inexperienced officer appeared on the screen displaying the rank of commander. The captain was shocked that the man had attained that rank so early, he appeared to be barely mid-way through his twenties. Just a sign of the times, he thought.

"E.D.F.S Hornet requests permission to dock," a rather authoritarian sounding voice came over the speakers.

"E.D.F.S Hornet, you are cleared for docking on bay 6, please be aware that some of the docking facilities are under repair, station operations will inform you of the current interim docking procedures." Ericsson had to say this to any ship wishing to dock with the station after the Krenarans took out all the docking ports during the battle, some were more damaged than others. Fortunately, work teams on-board had temporarily repaired bay 6.

"E.D.F.S Hornet understands and confirms, glad to be here echo base."

The communication ended, replaced by the image of the Hornet slowly advancing, the two smaller inter-system boosters of the three it possessed, briefly flared as they gently accelerated the ship for an instant before powering down. As it approached bay 6, small controlled bursts of reverse thrust from its forward thrusters, slowed the ship. Until finally with a deep 'thunk' its forward docking arm magnetically clamped onto the docking port.

A full diplomatic team arrived on the station, escorted by a squad from the 69th Sicarian guards.

Ericsson, Vargev and several other commanders had made their way to the docking area to formally greet the party.

"Welcome to echo base, ambassador......"

"Lataf," the ambassador corrected in a rather rude fashion. Vargev was already taking a dislike to this man, but said nothing.

Without a word the assembled men all began the walk to the nearest elevator.

"Where is the Krenaran representative?" he continued.

"He is in private quarters on-board the station, under guard. We have prepared an area to facilitate negotiations on the planet surface below," Ericsson replied.

"Very good, I shall prepare for the negotiations immediately."

"Quarters have been made available for your stay on deck 18."

"Thank you, captain."

With that, the ambassador left the assembled men, and headed to the elevator, with his entourage in tow.

"Who the hell does that guy think he is?" Vargev asked.

"An ambassador," Ericsson replied.

"I hate ambassadors, especially pricks like him."

Vargev and Ericsson returned to the command centre and waited for Lataf's signal, after several hours of waiting around for the ambassador, and Vargev becoming ever more frustrated with the man, the signal finally came that he was ready.

Ericsson and Vargev both returned to Lataf's quarters and met up with the escort party and the ambassador. "We will escort you to your shuttle, if you would follow me," Ericsson said.

"Of course."

The twelve strong party all made their way to the nearest available shuttle, Ericsson ushered them all inside, before taking a seat at the flight console. He keyed in a control that opened an internal comm. channel to the command centre.

"Shuttle echo six requests permission to disembark."

"Shuttle echo six, permission has been granted, good luck captain," the reply came over the speakers.

"Thank you, echo six out." Ericsson replied, we're going to need it, he thought.

The small shuttle gently lifted off and banked left as the gigantic hangar bay doors opened, revealing the inky blackness of space and the twinkling of distant stars. The silent forlorn wreckage of the starship graveyard confronted them as its inhabitants drifted aimlessly amongst themselves.

The shuttle accelerated out of the hangar bay and down towards the emerald hue of gamma IV far below. It began to shudder gently as the friction from the upper atmosphere buffeted the small craft, gradually it punched through the atmosphere and descended through the cloud cover, revealing to the occupants the scattered metallic wreckage, deep craters, and scarred landscape from the intense battle fought a week earlier.

"My god, what a mess," Lataf said indignantly.

Vargev harrumphed, but said nothing, instead using discretion as the better part of valour, never mind that hundreds of men had fought and died on that *mess* as he called it.

Ericsson bit his lip hard, feeling exactly the same way as Vargev did.

"Is there a problem captain?" The ambassador asked, baiting him.

"Well actually......" Ericsson went to say, then stopped in mid sentence. "No, no problem."

"Good, captain." The ambassador said with just a hint of sarcasm in his tone.

Ericsson silently berated himself for allowing the ambassador to get to him, it would not happen again. There were bigger things to consider here, like the peace treaty.

Dalvosh was due to arrive in a separate shuttle, and would be flanked by several Krenaran guards at the peace talks, making up the Krenaran contingent, this had already been arranged by Ericsson while they waited for Lataf to prepare.

The heavily damaged buildings of echo base were clearly visible now as the shuttle began its final approach into an area cleared of debris for their arrival. The gravitic engines thrummed into life, kicking up a plume of dirt and dust as they slowed the shuttle before it gently rested on its three hydraulic landing legs. A ramp gradually lowered as the shuttle powered down and the occupants all filed out into the damp and muddy surface.

The party slowly made their way towards the temporary headquarters set up for them, as they neared general Kalidis approached them, his nose still taped from the battering he took from Vargev, saluted and introduced himself to the ambassador. "I am General Georgiannos Kalidis, commander of this facility."

"What is left of it," the ambassador replied.

"If you would like to follow me I will show you to the negotiation area."

"Thank you general."

Kalidis joined the party and they continued on their way to the headquarters, just as the shuttle containing Dalvosh became visible over the horizon, before gently landing alongside the ambassadors own shuttle. The huge Krenaran emerged flanked by the shuttle pilot and about four or five E.D.F troops, Vargev couldn't make out the exact number as they were now some way off.

The ambassador's party approached the makeshift headquarters, there were two rather battle weary lieutenants guarding the entrance, who, nevertheless stood to attention and saluted the ambassador appropriately. Lataf however ignored the salute and pushed past these lieutenants, entering the wide, well lit interior.

This infuriated Ericsson who could hold his silence no longer. "You could have returned their salute ambassador," he said pointing back to the two guards stationed on the outside of the building.

"Why? I am not E.D.F, I am E.O.C.A." Lataf retorted matter of factly.

"It's about common courtesy and respect damnit! Many people have died here to make this possible." Ericsson shouted, beginning to lose his temper with the flagrantly disrespectful ambassador Lataf.

"And they will be honoured appropriately captain, my place is at the negotiating table, not at a battlefield."

At that Ericsson could say nothing.

The remainder of the ambassador's retinue all filed into the room, a few men were already there pointing small hand held cameras at them for the benefit of the outer colony news service, who were taking a deep interest in the talks. As they took their seats along the perimeter, Lataf and his aides sat at a large oval table which dominated the centre of the room, the ambassador began to quietly look over the terms of the treaty once again as he awaited Dalvosh's team.

Michael Alexander entered the room also, after taking time out from overseeing the repairs to the Liberty to be present at the talks. He sat down next to Vargev.

"Glad your back on your feet comrade," Vargev whispered to him.

"Thanks."

"How are the repairs going to the Liberty?"

"Not bad, considering I've got half the engineers of the base crawling over her, trying to get that bucket of bolts spaceworthy." He said with a wry smile.

A few minutes later and Dalvosh's team also entered the room, there were two other Krenarans who had joined him, as well as four

E.D.F troops who took up positions behind the Krenarans at the opposite periphery of the room.

Lataf was nervous and it showed. He had seen pictures of these aliens broadcast on the news during the fighting, but had never seen one up close until now. The sheer size, piercing red eyes, and reptilian features of these brutes that towered over him, was disconcerting to say the least.

Summoning all his inner strength and diplomatic training, he offered a rather shaky hand in friendship.

The Krenaran bowed his head as he shook it dutifully, Dalvosh's hand dwarfed his own and his handshake was as firm as iron. Lataf winced as his hand felt like it was being crushed and his arm shaken out of its socket.

Vargev quietly chuckled to himself in the corner of the room.

There was a printed hardcopy of the treaty on the table, as well as a digital copy stored on a data navigator, which Lataf held.

"The negotiations are now in session." Lataf said trying not to betray a hint of his nervousness as his aides made notes, another held a small recording device."

Dalvosh silently nodded, his eyes fixed on the ambassador. The news crew trained their cameras on the men.

"The terms of the Krenaran surrender, and subsequent ending of the E.O.C.A - Krenaran war are as such. Number 1, all military operations against E.O.C.A, its military arm the E.D.F, and E.O.C.A citizens and property must immediately cease."

"I understand and agree," Dalvosh replied calmly, betraying no emotion.

"Secondly, all Krenaran military assets, including troops, vessels, and related military equipment must immediately leave E.O.C.A territory."

Dalvosh agreed to this also.

"Thirdly, all human and Solarian prisoners of war must be returned to the closest E.O.C.A or Solarian colony world or facility where they can be returned to their appropriate homes and families."

Dalvosh also agreed to this, although somewhat reluctantly.

"There will be a three light year demilitarised zone, between E.O.C.A and Krenaran territories, extending 8 light years out from the Agemman colony and then across the north eastern tip of the connaught sector for another 15 light years as shown in your copy of the treaty."

An aide passed Dalvosh a copy of the treaty, which he eyed for a few moments before nodding in agreement.

"Any deviation from these terms will be considered either as an act of hostility towards the E.O.C.A government or an outright act of war."

Lataf gave Dalvosh and his aides some time to peruse the terms of the treaty.

An aide spoke up, it was Dalvosh's second in command, "you must not sign this pitiful excuse for a treaty Dalvosh, we can still win this war."

"Quiet Briax!" Dalvosh snapped, "If we lose the entire Krenaran race to win this war, what then? Who would be left to celebrate the great Krenaran victories? We cannot fight both the Terran and Solarian empires together."

Briax remained silent.

"A prudent course of action," Lataf said.

"I sign this treaty not for your pitiful sake, your race disgusts me. I sign this treaty for our son's sake, and their son's, and for the future of all Krenarans."

Dalvosh took the stylus and signed the declaration, Lataf then passed the Data navigator around the table, each aide in-turn then signed the treaty as a witness, before both Dalvosh and Lataf were handed their own copies. Eventually the hard copies were signed as well, Lataf picked up his own copy to return back to E.O.C.A headquarters on Earth.

"Today we have made history, let it be known that peace can be achieved on the field of battle and let peace return to the galaxy once more." A great loud cheer, reverberated around the room following this proclamation, at last, after almost a year of bitter fighting, the war was finally over. Humanity could get on with the task at hand, re-building and exploring the galaxy once again.

As the deliberations gradually drew to a close and the cameras switched off. A Solarian thrust his way into the room, Michael immediately recognised the former first officer of the Liberty. "Televis what are you doing here?"

"I've come from my ship in orbit with urgent news. Solarian intelligence has just made contact with a Krenaran agent. He killed three Solarian agents and severely injured a fourth. Before the last Solarian died, he revealed the Krenaran's codename as Lathiel."

"So the Krenarans propose peace, and then knife us in the back when we are not looking," Ericsson gave Dalvosh a look of disgust.

The two Krenaran aides rose up from the table, "we will tear your puny head off Terran!"

"Quiet!" shouted Dalvosh, "sit down all of you!"

The angry parties did as instructed, all looking towards the Krenaran commander, the human contingent with a look of barely concealed rage and betrayal, yet they listened anyway.

"I know of the agent known as Lathiel, he was our secret weapon, trained to be the perfect assassin, he is equipped with a biomechanical gland that secretes a specially formulated combat drug only recently discovered, the drug is called morphos x. It is what allows him to physically alter his appearance to match any humanoid upon contact. He is one of the most vicious and deranged of all Krenarans."

"Did you send him Dalvosh!" Vargev shouted, "because if you did, I swear your brain will coat the walls of this room!"

"How dare you accuse me of this!" Dalvosh shouted back, the two Krenarans made ready to charge Vargev and the humans present in the room, who all readied their weapons in response.

"Where is this assassin now!" Michael shouted over the din of angry raised voices. The Krenaran war threatened to re-ignite again at any moment.

"Last known location places him on Orion, reports suggest he is heading for Terra," Televis replied.

"There would be only one reason why Lathiel would be given an assignment on Terra," Dalvosh said. "He plans to kill your president."

"Orion is one weeks travel away from Earth," Ericsson said.

"Hell of a good time to activate your assassin Dalvosh, most of the E.D.F fleet is here, the main intelligence facilities at Sigma XI you destroyed eight months ago. No one to track him and no one to catch him," Vargev said accusingly.

"I swear on my honour as a Krenaran, I never activated Lathiel!" Dalvosh shot back.

"Then who did!" Ericsson shouted.

"Alax must have activated him before hostilities ended, he is the only one who would have had the authority."

"And we killed Alax over a week ago," Vargev said.

"So effectively we have a rogue agent, who doesn't know the war is over, on a mission to kill the President of E.O.C.A." Ericsson pointed out.

"That's about the size of it," Vargev replied.

"If this Lathiel succeeds in his mission, it could destabilise the entire peace process, war could break out all over again," Lataf announced.

"Is the Faeriath ready?" Ericsson asked.

"Negative, my ship is badly damaged from the battle, as is the remainder of the Solarian fleet. The rest of the Solarian warhost is at Agemman, Aurelias, and Eidolon, too far away to catch him in time."

"Which leaves…." Vargev said.

"The Liberty; we can catch him," Michael filled in for him.

"The Liberty's too badly damaged, it won't make it." Ericsson argued.

"Captain, I believe in the Liberty, and her crew. She'll make it," Michael countered.

"I hope she does captain, for all our sakes," Lataf said.

"I'm coming with you," Vargev said looking at Michael.

"As am I," Dalvosh also announced.

"What about your men here?" Briax said.

Vargev swung his Armschlager menacingly, its deadly barrel pointed directly at the Krenarans reptilian face. "I insist."

With that, the three of them dashed out of the makeshift headquarters towards the grounded Liberty.

Michael was first to touch his wrist comm. "Alexander to Kinraid, I want the Liberty prepped and ready to go, right now."

"The repairs aren't even complete cap'n, the new main engine isn't even tested yet."

"Too late commander we've run out of time, it's an emergency, Alexander out."

Vargev touched his wrist comm. too, "all commandoes in the area, I want a full squad, prepped and ready to ship out in five minutes, form up at the Liberty, Vargev out."

The three of them continued running, along broken tarmac roads and muddy wild grassland to where the Liberty rested.

Michael touched his wrist comm. once again, "Michael to Liberty, prepare to lift off as soon as we are aboard."

"Understood cap'n," the reply came.

The three of them reached the Liberty a few minutes later, where they found a full ten man squad of E.D.F commandoes stood to attention and a bewildered Logameier. "What is going on? Kinraid's just told me that the Liberty is taking off, repairs are nowhere near complete."

"Sorry Lieutenant, it's an emergency, we have to take off immediately."

"Then where are we going?"

"Earth, to stop an assassination plot against the president of E.O.C.A himself," Michael replied.

General Kalidis caught up with them, out of breath, he wheezed. "You're going to need me with you, to make sure this bucket of bolts holds together."

"You're welcome to come along," Michael replied as he climbed inside the port access hatch.

"Think your man enough for it Kalidis?" Vargev asked, then followed it up by simply saying, "click, click."

Kalidis frowned at the Russian and climbed onboard, followed by Dalvosh.

"Commandoes on me!" Vargev barked out his order.

The colonel and the remainder of the commandoes climbed onboard also.

Michael was soon on the bridge, in his somewhat muddied naval uniform. The bridge itself was still damaged in places and still bore many of the scars of the damage the ship had sustained.

"Status report," Michael asked as he took his seat.

"We have main power at seventy percent, ninety percent emergency power; all stations report ready," Kinraid replied.

Michael noticed that Eldathar was seated in the pilots chair again, "good to have you back ensign," he said as he placed a reassuring arm on the Solarian's slender shoulder. "Now let's get this show on the road!"

"Gravitic engines to maximum," Kinraid said.

Outside of the ship the grass swirled, whipped up by the force generated by the Liberties powerful gravitic engines propelling the ship skywards, a loud whine became audible as the anti-gravity motors struggled to keep the Liberty airborne.

"Retract landing legs," Michael said.

Eldathar responded, and the landing legs slowly retracted into their horizontal positions, matt black panels slit into position over them with a gentle creak.

"Main engines at one half power, we don't want to tax them too much just yet."

"Understood captain," Eldathar replied.

As the Liberty continued to ascend skyward, Televis, Ericsson and Lataf silently watched from the doors of the tank factory.

"Godspeed," they said in unison as the Liberty flew out of sight.

"Status of main engines," Michael said as the Liberty continued to climb through the atmosphere.

Kinraid constantly kept his eye on an engineering systems console at the rear of the bridge. "Main engines are okay so far, but at this speed we won't break orbit."

"Increase power to eighty percent," Michael said growing tense, the Liberty *had* to break free from the gravitational pull of Gamma IV, if not they were all doomed, and so was the E.O.C.A president.

"Increasing power," Eldathar replied.

The ship began to shudder as the gravitational forces and atmospheric pressures of the planet began to take their effect, Kinraid made his way over towards his usual seat and strapped himself in, this was proving to be a rather bumpy ride.

"We are approaching the upper atmosphere; main engine at seventy percent power and rising," Eldathar informed the bridge crew.

Down in engineering Kalidis and Logameier were working furiously. "Secure that panel" Logameier barked out over the noise. "Keep an eye on the status of the main engine in case it heats up too fast or gets too hot."

Solarian engineering crews literally ran from console to console, checking over vital systems.

The outer hull began to heat up as friction from the violent upper atmosphere of the planet continued to increase, the shuddering and swaying of the ship rose in its violence, flames scorched its outer hull as the atmospheric forces increased in their intensity.

Some of the plating used to seal the breach of the Liberties destroyed torpedo launcher began to buckle and tear under the pressures exerted upon it. The violent shuddering continued relentlessly as the small ship climbed higher and higher into the upper atmosphere of Gamma IV, sparks erupted from damaged circuits and consoles exploded, sending glass showering across the bridge. Michael secretly prayed that his damaged ship would hold together.

"Engines at eighty percent!" Eldathar struggled over the noise.

The ship continued to race through the atmosphere, finally the forces threatening to tear the damaged ship apart became too much, and the plating around the breach of the torpedo launcher sheared off completely, flames poured into the damaged section which had already been sealed off as a precaution, however now heat was building rapidly inside as super heated plasma from the intense heat whirled around the sealed off section. If something wasn't done quickly, the bulkheads would collapse and the whole ship could be lost.

"Forcefield! Seal that breach now!" Michael shouted over the cacophony of consoles exploding, violent shaking and sparks flying across the bridge.

A forcefield shimmered into life protecting the damaged section from the ravages of the atmospheric pressure, for now at least.

"Forcefield is in place cap'n, but I don't think it'll hold for long!" Kinraid shouted back.

Sweat trickled down the sides of Michael's face from the rising heat and desperation, "just a few more seconds," he whispered over pressed lips. The shuddering reached a fever pitch, and just for an instant, Michael, along with most of the bridge crew closed their eyes.

The shuddering had ceased, it had become calm once again. Slowly Michael opened one eye, then the other, confirming they were still in one piece. All that was visible on the viewer was starlight, they had done it, they had broken free of Gamma IV. He let out a loud sigh of relief. "I would consider that a successful test," he said.

Kinraid nodded his approval and a broad smile opened across his features, more at his thankfulness at still being alive than anything else.

"Set course for Earth, bearing zero-three-five degrees, elevation zero; best possible speed."

The Liberty leapt into plasma drive; destination Earth.

10. Earth race.

Location : Delta base.
Date : 18th October 2071.
Time : 21:44 hours.

The Krenaran assassin known as Lathiel casually walked towards the vast docking area of Delta base, replete with buggies and carts whizzing to and fro, loading and unloading supplies from ships that had come from all over E.O.C.A territory.

Although the majority of military vessels were taking part in the fighting around Gamma IV, some were still present providing a defence for the station and the colony world of Orion IV far below, others were undergoing emergency repair work, obviously damaged in combat in some other area of E.O.C.A space.

The majority of ships docked were transports, carrying vital medical and other supplies to civilians caught up in the huge conflict.

There was a small warship that the Terrans called a Ghandhi class destroyer, however he ruled out hitching a ride aboard it, it was doubtful he could overcome its crew, and even if he could, he wouldn't be able to control all the ship's systems himself.

A nice, small, inconspicuous transport would suffice for this mission. The trick was getting on-board without being detected however.

Three E.D.F naval officers walked straight past him, not paying him any heed whatsoever, just a few minutes before he had killed Ensign Butler with a knife straight through the back, nice and quiet, it had allowed him close contact with his body which he touched and then activated his crodes gland buried deep beneath his thick ribcage. It secreted the top secret combat drug known as morphos x, the drug caused him extreme pain as his body altered to take on the form of any humanoid he touched, but he had learned to cope with it.

He was his races ultimate weapon to bring down the puny Terrans once and for all. His mission was the elimination of the E.O.C.A president, a Terran by the name of James Rushfeldt.

The hated Solarians had managed to expose his mission on Perseus; he had barely escaped alive. Worst of all, the Solarian agents had managed to send a communiqué to Solarian command before he had disposed of them.

The Terrans would be waiting for him on Terra, he would have to be careful.

He made his way over to one of the docked transports, being careful not to attract any attention, a lone officer was standing guard at the docking port.

Transports didn't have as tight security as the warships of the E.D.F navy, this transport with a crew of only twelve, allowed him to take control of the ship with minimal difficulty. This small oversight was going to cost the Terrans very dearly indeed.

The young officer addressed him, "eello ensign, what are you doing here?"

"Ensign Butler transferring from the E.D.F.S Avenger," Lathiel replied.

The officer looked perplexed, "for what reason?"

Lathiel had to think quickly, "as an engineering assistant."

"Do you have your I.D. card?"

"Yes, here you are." Lathiel produced the I.D. card he had taken from the *real* ensign Butlers body.

The officer studied the card, before placing it into a reader to his right.

He used his Krenaran training to calm his nerves, but still readied himself in case anything should go wrong. After what seemed like an eternity, the officer finally said. "O.K. your all clear, welcome aboard the transport blue-177 ensign." He handed him back the card, as Lathiel went to embark on the transport, the officer asked. "Where are your transfer documents?"

Panic gripped Lathiel, "Still being processed, you know how it is," he replied meekly.

"Yeah don't I, you're probably right, thanks ensign," the officer said as he nodded knowingly at him.

Lathiel inwardly sighed with relief as he quietly stepped onboard the transport, once inside he found the confines tight and uncomfortable for his frail Terran body. The corridors were narrow and for the most part, badly lit. The transport seemed quiet, he surmised that no one else was yet onboard.

He walked up to a small computer display, the screen was cracked in one corner and the system looked ancient, however he did manage to access the crew manifest.

The transport was commanded by a Lieutenant Pryce, obviously the E.D.F didn't place as high a value on its transports as it did its warships, which would be why only a junior officer commanded the vessel, another costly oversight.

He exited the crew manifest and consulted the deck-plan, the ship had eight decks, four of them were given over to the enormous cargo hold. The remainder of the decks were taken up with the bridge, crew quarters, a small mess area, engineering, and a tiny medical bay as well as the main engines and thruster systems.

By consulting the deck-plan further, Lathiel noticed that there was a very small armoury located on the third deck, directly adjacent to the entrance to the cargo hold.

Exiting out of the manifest, he immediately began making his way there, quickly locating the cramped elevator to deck three. Once there he walked the length of the corridor, finally coming upon the door to the armoury on his left. There was a tiny swipe card reader to the side of the steel door.

Lathiel swiped the stolen I.D. card through the slot in the reader, and hoped it would give him access.

Success, a green light blinked on and he quietly entered the armoury.

There in the small room, barely larger than himself, and only dimly lit he noticed a rack of ten dusty looking pulse rifles and two heavy machine guns, together with a dozen or so combat knives.

It was prudent of the E.D.F to arm their transport crews, especially since the spate of Krenaran attacks on E.D.F transports in the last month, attempting to disrupt E.D.F supply lines. However, this time it allowed an assassin of the calibre of Lathiel to gain the upper hand.

The Krenaran agent weighed up the weapons, he had learned that the heavy machine guns were more powerful and had a faster rate of fire. However the pulse rifle was more accurate at range, he picked up a pulse rifle and grabbed two combat knives.

Lathiel had no idea whether he would actually use the pulse rifle or not as he was a master of close quarters fighting and could use those twin knives to devastating effect anyway.

After retrieving the weapons, he left the armoury as quietly as he entered and headed for the bridge.

After making it back to the elevator, he keyed in deck 1 for the bridge and was soon on the spartan looking command centre of the entire transport. He could blow the docking latches and launch the ship right now if he wanted, however a renegade ship like that would attract far too much attention and peregrine fighters would be swarming over his bow within minutes, better to wait until the transport gets under way officially.

As he looked over this dingy excuse for a command centre he noted the different stations, there was the rudimentary ships pilots console, the operations station, and the rather worn captains chair. Around the walls of this rectangular room were some small displays, there was a door to the side of the bridge that read 'captains quarters'.

He tried to open the door, however it had been locked out, instead he tried the pilots console, Lathiel needed to know where this ship was going. Hopefully the pilot had already plotted a flight plan into his console.

Lathiel accessed the console and found that indeed he had, this transport was heading to Barnards star to pick up medical supplies from a small facility there, and would be departing delta base at 09:00 hours tomorrow morning. It's a shame it will never make it there, he thought with an evil smile.

The Liberty was hurtling toward Earth at plasma factor 6.5, the ships maximum speed was plasma factor 7, however Kinraid had advised Michael that if they attempted that speed, the Liberties already weakened hull could start to give way.

"So, how does this morphos x drug work?" Michael asked Dalvosh.

"It is the result of several years of research in perfecting the ultimate assassin. It is secreted by a gland contained within Lathiels rib cage, it causes him extreme pain whenever it is used, but allows him to assume any humanoid form at will."

"So he could walk right into this command centre and change into any one of us."

"Yes, however he would have to have some form of physical contact first."

"Like what?"

"A pat on the back, a handshake, that sort of thing," Dalvosh replied. "However he does have one weakness."

"Which is?" Vargev asked after listening in to the conversation.

"His basic D.N.A structure remains Krenaran, and it can be picked up by any scanner capable of scanning D.N.A sequences."

"Like a Solarian scanner," Eldathar cut in.

"Exactly, that was why the Solarians present at Perseus picked him up," Dalvosh said nodding.

"Lucky for us we 'ave a few of those Solarian scanners aboard," Kinraid said.

"What's our status?" Michael asked.

"The ship's still in a bad way, te' damage we took getting into orbit will have to be repaired before we set down on Earth otherwise we will simply burn up in te' atmosphere," Kinraid replied.

"We'll have to make repairs on-route, we don't have time to stop at a repair facility." Michael said as he pressed a control on his wrist comm. "Alexander to Logameier."

"Logameier here captain, I'm a little busy right now, what's up?" replied the chief engineer, who was busily strengthening the weakened bulkheads around the destroyed torpedo launcher.

"Can you re-configure some Solarian scanners to be usable by humans?"

"I'll have a couple of the Solarian technicians take a look at them. Might I ask what for?" Logameier asked rubbing sweat from his brow, it was still warm in here from the heat build up after leaving the atmosphere. He really didn't need more tasks right now, it was taking every last minute of his time keeping the Liberty from falling apart.

"It's going to help us hunt some assassin," Michael smiled.

"I like the sound of that captain, I'll get some Solarian techs right on it."

"Good man," with that, Michael ended the transmission.

"Anything else I need to know about?" Michael asked, his hopes buoyed a little now that they had a way to track this little chameleon.

"Apart from the fact that Lathiel is lethal with both close combat and ranged weapons, and can melt into the background virtually anywhere, I can't think of a thing," Dalvosh replied with a hint of sarcasm, he knew the humans were out of their league in dealing with Lathiel right now.

"Riiight, nothing to worry about then," Michael replied, his hopes cruelly dashed again.

Vargev restrained a slight chuckle, he was actually beginning to like this Dalvosh. However on second thought, nope, he hated all Krenarans equally.

"Can't this thing go any bloody faster?" Michael asked, wanting to vent his frustration at something.

"Sorry captain, not without further damage to the ship," Eldathar replied from the pilot's chair.

The Liberty continued hurtling through the star-lit blackness of deep space.

Next morning Lathiel awoke early, he had stowed away in a dark disused area of the cargo hold, between some unknown crates. This frail Terran body ached from sleeping on the cold, hard floor. He slowly got to his feet, his eyes had developed a kind of crusty, powdery deposit in the corners either side of his Terran 'nose'. He had no idea what it was but knew that it irritated him, and so he rubbed at them with his finger, at once this annoying deposit had cleared.

He felt lethargic, and shook his head to release the fuzzy feeling, gradually feeling a little better and slightly more alert.

Making his way out of the cargo hold, he found that the ships crew or prey as he liked to think of them, had returned as they nonchalantly strode down the corridor past him completely oblivious to the danger he represented. Although his appearance altering drug caused him immense pain, he liked being able to pass unnoticed, being able to slip through virtually any net, all he had to do was kill someone, something which came very easily to him.

11. The mystery of transport blue-177.

Lathiel knew there would be problems, with such a small crew everyone knew everyone, so he had to keep to himself as much as possible. Since everyone was busily getting the ship ready for departure, he decided that he would hole up in a cramped, confined, gloomy maintenance access corridor on deck six for the time being.

"Hey Siccio!" One of the crewmen shouted.

Crewman Siccio walked over to him, "whassup Frankie?"

"You seen a weird looking guy walking around here lately?" crewman mike 'Frankie' Franklin asked.

"Nope, not a thing, why do you ask?"

"I saw a guy before, coming from the cargo hold. Never saw him before in my life."

"It's probably one of the loaders from the station, you know how people get moved about in this dumbass war, besides I heard something earlier about some new guy transferring over, might be him."

"Yeah, your probably right prettyboy."

Prettyboy was Siccio's nickname, ever since the crew used to make fun of how long he spent in the mirror, Siccio was the ships pilot and sometime helper, he modelled himself on the classic brylcreem boys of the 1950's and was vain to a fault.

Siccio left the cargo hold and headed back in the direction of the station, while 'Frankie' made his way towards the command centre. Once there he met up with the transports commanding officer, Lieutenant Pryce.

"What's our status?" he asked.

"All supplies have been stowed onboard, everyone is accounted for, Siccio has just popped over to the station to get his flightplan approved, then we should be all set."

"Good, as soon as Siccio returns I want to get underway," Pryce said nodding.

"Understood."

Half an hour later Siccio had returned, and the transport began to get underway.

"Contact Delta base control and request permission to depart," Pryce said as he settled in his cracked and worn command chair, letting out a small yawn, he had done this a thousand times, the monotony was unending.

"Delta base confirms," Frankie replied after a few seconds.

"Release docking hatch and back us away from the station, ten percent reverse thrust."

The crew complied and the comparatively tiny transport began to back away from the gargantuan station, navigation lights and the light from observation platforms played gently across the outer hull of the small vessel, its twin forward thrusters shot out streams of super heated hydrogen, forcing the vast bulk of the transport into reverse.

When the transport was clear, the rear thrusters briefly fired to kill the reverse motion, and then the rear port and front starboard thrusters fired simultaneously to gradually turn the transport away from the facility.

Once a safe distance away, its much more powerful inter-system engines blazed into life and accelerated the transport away from the station.

Lathiel crouched motionless in the maintenance corridor, he could feel the ship accelerate through the gentle vibrations in the deck plating under his feet. He knew his time had almost come, they would soon enter into plasma drive; and then he would act.

The transport continued on its course away from the station, until what was a gigantic near spherical structure with its outer defence perimeter surrounding it like an enormous halo, was just a tiny metallic gleam, glinting far in the distance.

Finally, Pryce gave the command with all of the tiny amount of enthusiasm he could muster, "activate plasma drive."

Siccio keyed in the controls and a single incandescent beam of bright blue energy shot forth from the transports plasma emitter and opened the familiar swirling energy of the plasma wake directly ahead of the transport.

"Enter plasma drive," Pryce said.

The ships inter-system engines roared once more, and it gradually disappeared inside the wake, the energy quickly collapsing behind it.

"Now it's this all the way to Barnards star." Pryce said, slouching in his command chair.

Lieutenant Pryce was a full blooded E.D.F naval officer, or that was what he thought, he should be serving on one of the huge and powerful warships of the fleet patrolling the front lines, getting in on the action.

Instead, he commanded this flying rust bucket, it was degrading. Truth be known, Lieutenant Samuel Pryce wasn't nearly as clever as he thought he was, poor results at the academy meant that he wasn't chosen to be a serving officer in the fleet, and when war broke out he was posted to this transport vessel, dashing his dreams of front line action overnight.

Only when the elderly former commander Ben Howard died four months ago, was he even placed in command of the ship.

As soon as the transport had leapt into plasma drive Lathiel acted, he cautiously made his way along the tight confines of the maintenance corridor, stopping at the hatch at the end, gently pressing his ear against its cold steel. He could hear nothing, so he took a calculated risk and quietly forced the hatch open. The corridor was clear.

Replacing the hatch, he continued to cautiously advance down a larger, more brightly lit corridor. He could hear footsteps approaching, looking around the corridor, he noticed a door was ajar. Diving into a smelly, dimly lit room, he silently unsheathed his stolen knives. The room happened to be a communal toilet block, he entered a cubicle and closed the door behind him.

"Man I gotta pee," a voice said as its owner noisily burst into the room, the sound of footsteps went past the cubicle and stopped. The familiar sound of a zipper being undone and then liquid splashing against a hard surface gave Lathiel all the clues he needed.

While the man was busily relieving himself, Lathiel silently and very gently opened the cubicle door. The man had his back to him, taking great care Lathiel silently stalked the man.

His target, completely unaware of his impending doom went to zip himself back up, when he felt a sharp, agonizing, searing pain in his lower back, as though something had bitten into him. His hand went to feel the source of the pain, and it returned slick with blood.

He staggered around, and to his incredulity saw another E.D.F officer, smiling, and brandishing a combat knife, coated in blood.

As the mans vision began to fade, he spluttered. "you?.....who the hell are.....you." The victim gave up his struggle for consciousness and flopped face first onto Lathiel, who picked up the man in a firemans lift and seated the body on the toilet.

"Death," Lathiel replied with a sadistic grin, gently brushing his hand on the man's pale cheek as he activated his crodes gland. With a roar of agonizing pain, slowly but surely took on the form of the man he had just murdered in cold blood.

He took the I.D. card from the corpse and learned that the mans name was Bryan Fletcher, and was another engineering assistant. Lathiel gently closed the cubicle door on the corpse of the *real* Bryan Fletcher.

The Krenaran assassin washed his bloodstained knife in the toilet sink, hid them back inside his uniform, and left the toilet. One down, eleven to go, he thought as he headed to engineering, eager not to arouse any undue suspicion.

The transport continued on its journey through the swirling vortex of plasma drive. On the command centre, Siccio was making minor course corrections and Lieutenant Pryce was getting increasingly bored. However down in engineering Lathiel was already planning his next move.

"At last, glad you could join us, how long does it take to go for a piss," a dark skinned man said.

Lathiel guessed the man to be in his forties, he was slightly greying at the sides of his short fuzzy looking hair, and he didn't like the mans tone. Something he would remedy later, however at this moment in time he was stood in the middle of a wide-open engineering bay and there were witnesses.

"Listen Fletcher, the main power conduit on deck seven has come loose again, things a pain in the ass. I need you to go help Jackson fix it."

"Yes sir," Lathiel replied.

"You feeling okay Fletcher?" The man asked.

"Yes sir, why do you ask?"

"Because you never call me sir it has always been lieutenant."

"Sorry lieutenant," Lathiel replied, mentally chastising himself.

With that, he left engineering and headed straight for deck seven, a few minutes later and after a short journey on the elevator, he had arrived.

Finding that there was no power anywhere on the deck, Lathiel's Terran eyes found it hard to adjust to the gloom, however he could just about see the beam from Jackson's torch in the distance.

Lathiel drew his knife again, and steadily advanced, like a panther stalking its prey, waiting for the exact moment to make the kill.

Jackson was busy working on the coupling, the conduit had worked its way loose from a vital connection. It was to be expected, he thought. The ship was nearly thirty years old after all.

He heard movement behind him, in blind panic he whirled around, his heart thumping, sweeping his torch left and right, the surrounding supports and bulkheads threw off a myriad of shadows as the torchlight swept over it, his eyes strained in the dark. There was nothing. Jeez Jackson, get a grip, the sooner this damned power coupling is fixed the sooner the lights come back on, he thought.

"Hey Fletcher, is that you!" He shouted down the corridor, just in case. There was no answer.

"Where the hell is that asshole," Jackson mumbled to himself.

Lathiel had secreted himself behind a small support girder a few feet away from Jackson. He gently adjusted his grip on the knives so that the blades pointed inwards following the contours of his forearm, and slowly approached the doomed Terran.

As Lathiel approached, Jackson spun around to face him. "Jesus, Fletcher don't creep up on me like that," he said as his hand clung to his chest.

He was jumpy, nervous, Lathiel was enjoying this, without another word, the Krenaran assassin swung the concealed knife upwards and outwards in a wide arc, catching and slicing open Jacksons throat.

He dropped his torch and fell to his knees gurgling, spluttering, and clutching at his ruined throat, to help the man on his way Lathiel gripped the mans neck, and with a sharp twist broke it. Jacksons body fell face first on the floor, motionless.

Lathiel quietly picked up the torch and scanned the corridor for a door. There was one on his right, about ten metres ahead.

Dragging the blood soaked body into the room, he found it was a very small sickbay, and was deserted. The entire deck was until they got the power back online down here. Shining his torch around the room, Lathiel could only see a single bed, it would have to do. He hauled the limp body of Jackson onto it, before cleaning his knives again and exiting the room.

Re-sheathing and hiding the blades back inside his uniform, Lathiel headed back the engineering section, three decks above.

Once there, the dark skinned man greeted him again, "Hey Fletcher, you fixed that coupling I told you about?"

"Yes lieutenant," Lathiel lied.

"Where's Jackson?"

"Oh, he's just finishing up, getting the tools together," Lathiel lied again.

"Couldn't you have helped him?"

Lathiel knew this man had a dislike for him from the tone of his voice, and from his posture as the man disrespectfully turned his back on him. He did a quick scan of the room, nobody else was here, it was just the two of them, and time for a little sweet revenge. Lathiel drew one of his knives, and before the man even had a chance to turn around he threw the blade with such force straight at him, the knife whistled through the air.

The man staggered forward as he felt the impact of the blade embed itself in the back of his skull. His eyes began to roll, and he began foaming at the mouth as he desperately clutched at the blade protruding from the back of his head to no avail. Finally, his legs buckled and he collapsed with a thud onto his back. His head snapped back and slammed into the deck plating, forcing the knife ever deeper inside his skull, until the very tip of the blade was faintly visible protruding through his forehead.

"Maybe that will teach you some respect," Lathiel spat at the corpse as he dragged the body into a side room taking care to seal the door shut behind him. Only nine more to go, he thought with a sadistic grin.

Siccio arrived in the toilet block and immediately noticed one of the cubicles was busy, there was no sound coming from the cubicle though which was strange. One of the crew might have fallen asleep on the toilet, he thought.

After relieving himself he asked, "You okay in there buddy?"

Siccio didn't know whether to open the door or not, after waiting a few seconds he bit the bullet and forced the door open.

The pale form of Ensign Fletcher stared blankly at him.

"Damn man! You could have said something!" Siccio said, angered at the ignorance of the man slumped in front of him.

The body slowly gave way, and flopped off the toilet seat, leaving a crimson smear along the cistern.

"Holy shit!" Siccio panicked, as terror gripped him, his heart pounded in his chest, dashing out of the toilet block and into the corridor, wanting to be anywhere but back in there. He sprinted back to the command centre to tell Lieutenant Pryce the grisly news.

Back in engineering Lathiel had reverted to the form of the man he had just killed, looking at his I.D. card his name was Lieutenant Junior Grade Wesley Forrest. He was the ships chief engineer. Unsure of his next move, he decided to take a walk through the ship waiting for a target to present itself.

Finally it did, in the form of a rather attractive dark haired young woman, heading toward the mess area, it was almost a shame he had to kill her. Lathiel elected to calmly follow the woman, another crewmember walked past them; greeting him informally.

The two of them arrived at the mess area, Lathiel sat down and quietly observed. The woman proceeded to order some disgusting smelling Terran food from a simplistic, battered looking food synthesiser; he was hard pushed not to be sick. However, he deigned to push such thoughts to the back of his mind. He had a mission to complete and nothing was going to stop him.

He made his way toward the machine as if going to order something himself.

"Oh hello Wesley, is everything going okay down in engineering?" The woman asked politely.

"Perfectly," Lathiel replied, resisting the urge to sneer.

"Oh good, I suppose that's one thing to be grateful for at least," The woman said as she moved to walk away from the machine and sat down at a table not too far away.

As he was pretending to order the food, he ever so gently unsheathed one of his blades, and as he walked past the seated woman; rammed it straight through the back of her chair. The woman lurched forward under the force of Lathiels powerful thrust, blood spurted across the table from her mouth and she flopped forward into her food. Lathiel retrieved the knife and calmly left the mess area.

Siccio had now arrived on the bridge, panting and panicking. "Lieutenant!"

Pryce could see the man was in a state, "calm down Siccio, what's wrong?"

"It's Fletcher, he's been murdered." Siccio gasped, his heart still racing. "How?"

"Looks like someone's stabbed him," he said.

"Let's go; Chambers, set the ship to computer control."

Pryce, Chambers, and Siccio all left the command centre, and made their way to the toilet block to see the body for themselves.

"I swear, I'll have whoever's done this blown out the airlock," Pryce said as they headed to the elevator.

A few minutes later, they had arrived at the grisly scene.

Pryce checked over the body, "He's been stabbed alright, in the lower back. He wouldn't have even seen his attacker; poor bastard." He turned to face Siccio, "since at this moment, you are the prime suspect, I'm placing you under house arrest for murder, until we can rule you out as a suspect."

"But I didn't do it!" Siccio protested.

"You were the first one on the scene, are there any other witnesses that can provide an alibi?"

"Well, err, no. But I swear I didn't kill Fletcher! I was taking a piss for Christ sake!"

"Chambers, lock him in the forward hold until we can find out who did this."

Chambers advanced on Siccio, who pleaded once again. "Pryce, you've gotta believe me, I didn't do this!" He said pleading as he pointed to the body.

"Sorry man," Chambers said as he ushered an irate Siccio out of the door.

"You believe me, don't you?" Siccio asked, as Chambers continued to lead him away.

"For my part, yes, I believe you," Chambers acknowledged. "But you know better than I do, rules are rules, I don't like it but I have to follow it. You were the first on the scene, and you have no one who can back up your story. Standard E.D.F policy dictates that you are the prime suspect until proven otherwise."

"Damned E.D.F rules, I liked it more when we were civilian."

"Blue-177 is a Lincoln class supply ship, built by the E.D.F, maintained by the E.D.F, And ultimately governed by the E.D.F, sorry man." Chambers repeated as they headed to the forward hold.

Lathiel arrived on the bridge, strangely it was deserted. He quickly checked over the room and the captain's quarters, not a soul in sight, the ship was flying under computer control.

This presented a unique opportunity, he thought as he studied the dirty, scratched computerised displays lining certain areas of the oval perimeter.

Finally he came across a control that sealed the bridge doors shut in-case the ship was boarded. With a sadistic grin, Lathiel keyed in the controls and with a heavy metallic clunking noise the bridge door interlocks closed.

Soon stage one of my mission will be complete, he thought as he glanced over the environmental systems monitor and began to experiment with the controls. Finally he pressed the activate button.

Along the entire length of the port and starboard sides of the transport, exhaust vents slowly opened, and began venting the ships oxygen out into space. The remaining crewmen on board gasped for breath as the deadly vacuum of space sucked the air out of the vessel. Temperatures plummeted, as lieutenant Pryce, crewmen Franklin and Chambers, Siccio, and everyone else on the ship all fell to their knees, as they slowly, horribly, suffocated before gently freezing to death.

Lathiel was protected from venting the oxygen from the ship, through the act of sealing off the bridge earlier, effectively creating a separate environment within the room. He calmly waited seven or eight minutes, just to be absolutely certain that everyone else onboard was dead.

"Ah at last, a little peace and quiet," he smiled to himself as he keyed in the controls, returning the exhaust vents to their original positions.

Making his way to the pilot's position, he strapped himself in, and calmly plotted in a new course. Zero-six-seven degrees, elevation zero, straight for earth.

On the Liberty, Captain Michael Alexander was attempting to tune into the outer colony news service, to get a glimpse of what he had to expect on Earth. They were two days into the journey now, and had just passed through the Wolf 359 system.

Finally he had found the correct frequency, and in a small corner of the cracked display the video feed from the outer colony news service flickered into existence.

"I am Annika Raumov; this is the outer colony news service. The top stories today; it has now been two days since the historic Gamma IV peace treaty was signed between a team of E.O.C.A diplomats, and the Krenaran military, bringing peace to the war ravaged outer colonies. Celebrations and street parties continue to take place on colony worlds across E.O.C.A territory as news of the peace treaty spreads. In three days time, E.O.C.A president James Rushfeldt will be giving a speech broadcast throughout the colony worlds, congratulating the valiant struggles of the military, the population, and the spirit of humanity. There will also be a two minute silence to remember the greatest loss of life humanity has suffered since the second world war over one hundred and twenty five years ago. There will also be a warning about the tough times still to come, as the devastated outer colonies begin to re-build."

"That is when he'll strike," Dalvosh said, his lumbering form hunched over Michael.

"Then we'll have to make sure that he doesn't." Michael said as he continued to study the display, "do you have any other information that might help us with this guy?"

"Not really, I wasn't at the facility where he was trained, all that I know is that he's an expert assassin who has a specially created bio-technological gland that secretes this morphos x into his bloodstream. This gland also has a memory that keeps his original Krenaran D.N.A in a state of suspended animation. So that he can revert back to his Krenaran form. Ultimately, the stresses of changing shape and bone structure will kill him, but by then the damage will have already been done."

"Tough break, so basically he is expendable," Vargev said.

"Yes, Lathiel is just an experiment, if he proved successful we were going to recruit more subjects in an attempt to eliminate your highest value targets."

"Jesus, if the war didn't end when it did, we could be looking at hundreds of Lathiels," Michael said.

Dalvosh silently nodded, his reptilian eyes almost giving away a hint of sadness at the level his people had sank to.

"Just how much of an expert is this guy?" Vargev asked.

"There are rumours amongst the higher ranks in the Krenaran military, that he can approach, kill you, and then disappear before you even knew he was there," Dalvosh replied.

"Then I guess that the odds are not on our side," Michael said rubbing his temples.

"I would say not."

Lathiel was sat alone in the pilot's chair of the now captured E.D.F Lincoln class transport blue-177. He grew weary, he was weary of the simplistic, cumbersome nature of Terran shipping. Indeed, Terran ships were grand and massive, but they were also awkward, and slow to maneuver, on top of that they had a woeful top speed. It was no wonder, he thought, that Krenaran ships had decimated scores of them.

He was just passing the Barnards star system, and was only three days away from his destination. Three days until the weakling E.O.C.A president dies, and the Terrans will have no choice but to surrender to Krenaran superiority. Then he could go back to his home on the Krenaran moon of Klymar, a rich man. He had heard no word from his lord Alax on Gamma IV, Lathiel presumed that he was either still fighting the Terran ships around that area, or that he had finally claimed the large Terran base there and would resume contact soon, the thought heartened him. Somehow Lathiel doubted that the pitiful resistance offered by the Terrans and the hated meddling Solarians, would stop the overlord of the Krenaran empire.

Alax had once visited the top secret training facility on Corvandris, and in his Krenaran form Lathiel was slightly taller than average, standing at just over 9 feet tall. But even he was in awe of the size and power Alax exuded on those powerful mechanical legs of his. He was the epitome of raw Krenaran strength and power.

Strangely though, it wasn't Alax himself who had sent him on this mission, it was another high ranking Krenaran officer by the name of Galdon. Lathiel had managed to check this Galdon's clearance before departing for Terran space. And it was definitely high, he had level ugro access codes, and only a member of Alax's personal staff had that high a level.

Lathiel, who's real name was Krovash, a name that only Alax and Axus had known, although Axus was killed. This was intentional, for fear of it leaking out into public knowledge.

He had spent his early years with his father Vugron, who was a Krenaran foot trooper, the young Krovash desperately wanted to follow in his fathers glorious footsteps. To be in the Krenaran military was one of the most powerful positions a Krenaran could obtain. It granted housing, land, even political power. Indeed, the head of the Krenaran military is widely judged to be the head of the Krenaran race.

Vugron, however never got to that lofty height, he was just an ordinary rank and file soldier. He had his small house on Gravosh III, he had his family, and that was all that his father wanted in life, and this was where the young Krovash grew up.

However, things were to change when Krovash came of age to join one of the many Krenaran military academies, he knew very early on that he was destined for some other purpose.

In Krovash's training, he would never accept that a frontal charge using brute force and with all weapons blazing was the answer. Much to the chagrin of his superiors, instead Krovash repeatedly opted to attack from the shadows, to blend in with his surroundings, and to strike when his enemy was at his most vulnerable. Many thought Krovash's techniques were superior, however military commanders viewed it as a cowardly affront to the pride and power of their military, Krenarans skulking in dark corners like frightened children, never.

It was this tendency that ultimately unsettled the warriors within his company, many thought it an insult to the Krenaran sense of honour and pride in combat. This led to him being given the title Gromish alcra, the sword from the dark.

His company commander however, recognised his talents and transferred the young warrior to the newly operational top secret training facility on Corvandris. Where, for many years he perfected the art of striking from the shadows, as well as from distance; to kill without ever being seen.

It was this innate ability led to him being selected for this most dangerous of missions.

Three days later, the transport blue-177 finally entered the Sol system. Lathiel, with consummate skill dropped the ship out of plasma drive on the far side of the moon. He wanted to get as far in-system on plasma drive as he could. Thereby shortening the time in which the pathetic E.D.F could react to his intrusion.

A communication blazed through the speakers, interrupting his concentration. "Transport blue-177, this is lunar control, state your reason for approach?"

Lathiel had to think hard, and quickly. "Lunar control, this is transport blue-177, we are on approach to Earth to deliver medical supplies from Barnards star." He managed to remember from the late Siccio's flightplan.

"Transport blue-177, you are earlier than scheduled. Can you give any satisfactory reason?"

Lathiel grew anxious, if he didn't give the correct response now, within five minutes fighters would be all over him picking him apart. "Lunar control, we were loaded faster than anticipated at Barnards star."

A long pause ensued, which only served to heighten the tension. Finally, a communication broke the silence. "Transport blue-177, you are cleared for approach to Earth."

Never had Lathiel felt such relief at hearing that news, he gently increased the power to the ships inter-system engines which roared into life, and the transport gradually picked up speed and headed towards Earth itself, the inter system boosters blazing white hot.

Barely half an hour later, the battered Liberty dropped out of plasma drive near alpha base, orbiting mars.

"Get me alpha base command," Michael said, he had no time for pleasantries.

"Admiral Mason here, welcome back Liberty, I've heard great things happened over at Gamma IV."

"Sorry admiral we are here on business, it's an emergency. Have there been any unusual events happening around Earth?"

"Not around Earth captain, there was an E.D.F transport that came in out of plasma drive near the lunar control station. I found it a little odd, since transports don't usually drop out of plasma drive this far inside a system and it was much earlier than expected."

Michael grew tense, half an hour. That would mean it would be getting ready to dock at Earth.

"What was the identification of the transport?" Michael asked.

Mason consulted something off-screen for a few seconds, "blue-177, what kind of emergency captain?"

"There is going to be an assassination attempt on the president at his speech today, do you know where it is taking place?"

"Sure, everyone knows. It's in Prague, at the institute of quantum mechanics. Due to start in about an hour and a half's time, what proof of this do you have captain?"

The huge form of Dalvosh stomped into view of the admiral, "The threat is real admiral, he is a rogue agent activated before the war ended, and he can take on the form of any humanoid he touches; only we can stop him."

"My god!" The admiral gasped, "I'll contact Earth, let them know of the situation, and get you emergency landing clearance."

"I would recommend alerting your guards quietly, if Lathiel notices any sign of increased activity, it could spook him," Dalvosh suggested.

"Understood; Mason out," the communication ceased.

"Continue on course for Earth, maximum sub-light." Michael said, preying that they weren't too late.

"Yes captain." Eldathar replied working the controls.

The Liberty rapidly accelerated past the gigantic spherical installation of alpha base, and headed for Earth.

The small transport had cut through Earth's atmosphere with relative ease, and continued to descend through the cloud cover towards a freight loading platform, just outside of Prague.

The speakers blazed into crackled life once again, "Transport blue-177 you are cleared to dock at pad D, once docked please have your crew remain onboard for security checks."

"Understood control," Lathiel replied before he ended the communication. They won't find anyone aboard, he thought. Just corpses, which, while they are busy trying to find out what has happened I'll be slipping straight out the front door.

The twinkling lights of the city of Prague were visible now as the transport gently glided on its final approach toward the platform.

Lathiel kept his eyes peeled on the viewer as he tried to make out the shape of the platform amongst the sprawl of buildings. Gradually it revealed itself; just on the outskirts of the city.

Quickly keying in some controls on the pilots console, five landing legs gently lowered from their positions secreted within the underside of the transports hull.

The small ship continued to slow and descend for its final approach to the platform. Lathiel keyed in the control to add reverse thrust as the transport came in, and gradually slowed the ship until it virtually hovered above the landing pad using just the power from its gravitic engines. He killed the power just as the transport came to rest on the pad. Lights from the surrounding buildings shone down upon the transports aged hull.

Lathiel, still in the guise of lieutenant Forrest, went to greet the cargo inspectors. Making his way through the tight confines of the ship and down towards the lower loading ramp on deck seven. He punched in a control and lowered the main ramp with a loud hiss of pressurised air. Once the ramp had finished lowering, three men came aboard. Lathiel acknowledged the men with a polite nod "Lieutenant Forrest, bringing in those medical supplies as requested."

"Forrest, where the hell is the commander here, you're three days early! We might have to turn you around, does he even know how much shit he is in! He's damned well screwed up our schedule for the next three days."

Another man spoke up, "There's another transport due in on this pad in a few hours time and we'll have to divert him, which throws the others out."

"Just following my orders," Lathiel said, trying to remain as blank as possible.

Two of the three men headed towards the command deck in an attempt to find the now dead commander, lieutenant Pryce.

"You can check through the inventory with me," the third man said, he was a shade taller than the other two, with a rather scruffy looking unkempt beard.

"No problem," Lathiel said with a smile, his chance had now come.

The Liberty closed in on Earth, just passing the moon.
"Get me E.D.F command headquarters on Earth," Michael asked.
"Patching ye' in," Kinraid replied.
A young woman with long dark brown locks flickered up on the holoviewer, "greetings Liberty, what can we do for you."
"I need full emergency landing clearance in Prague, preferably as close to the institute of Quantum mechanics as you can get us."

"We have already been informed of the situation through E.D.F command, you intend to physically land a ship the size of the Liberty next to the institute?" She asked incredulously.

"Or as close as we can get," Michael finished for her.

The woman consulted something out of view for a few seconds.

"There's a park near to the facility that you might be able to land in. It's called Stromoika park, I'll arrange for the area to be cordoned off immediately."

"Thanks," Michael replied, "Liberty out."

"Well here goes," Kinraid said.

Vargev gave the commander a look of silent distain; he must be a newbie to come out with something like that.

"Everyone hold onto something, this is going to be rough," Michael said.

That enticing sapphire blue planet, with gentle wisps of white cloud that was the Earth loomed large, the bright azure glow of its atmosphere was clearly visible as the Liberty began its entry.

The outer hull began to heat up rapidly, and the ship started to shudder, at first gently then increasing in violence as the winds in the upper atmosphere increased.

Michael preyed that the ship would make it through entry, she had taken a heck of a lot of damage, and it would be touch and go.

The Liberties hull trailed fire and smoke as it punched ever deeper into Earths atmosphere. The shuddering became almost unbearable; conduits exploded and crewmen were thrown across the floor. Small fires began to break out amongst the damaged circuitry, the fire suppression system was knocked offline again. Outside the ship it looked like a travelling inferno, parts of damaged hull plating were torn completely off the ship due to the immense pressure.

Even the huge form of Dalvosh was struggling against the unrelenting violence of punching deeper and deeper into the Earth's atmosphere.

The shuddering had finally stopped, smoke still hung thick across the command centre, and the crew immediately went to work putting out the myriad of small fires. At length, the environmental systems came back online and started clearing the smoke.

Michael wiped the sweat lining his brow, "We made it!" Elated, a wide grin played across his face. It was all he could do to stop himself punching the air in delight, damn I love this ship, he thought.

The holoviewer cleared, showing the white blanket of cloud cover below them, the ship continued to descend trailing smoke and pieces of damaged hull plating from its incredibly hot outer hull.

"Status?" Michael asked as the rest of the command crew picked themselves up from the violence of entry.

"We've got severe damage to the outer hull; multiple hull fractures. Integrity is at eighteen percent and holding, minor injuries reported."

"Well at least we made it through," Michael said with genuine relief.

The Liberty quickly punched through the cloud cover, and flew over the landmass that was mainland Europe.

They descended quickly, and soon they could see the mountain ranges between them and the outskirts of Prague itself.

Lathiel silently approached the form of the man checking through the transports inventory, he had his back to him, consulting a handheld scanner. Before the poor soul even had a chance to react, the assassin grabbed his head, wrenched it backwards and savagely sliced the mans throat. The man staggered, coughing and spluttering on his own blood, Lathiel thought the man was making too much noise in his death throes so he rammed the mans head against a large shipping container next to him, instantly knocking him unconsciousness.

Carefully, he dragged the man's body behind some other containers and activated his crodes gland again, pain ravaged the assasins body once more as he gradually took over the form of the inventory man, within seconds the transformation was complete.

The impostor searched through the bloodied, lifeless body, took the man's I.D. card and wiped any trace of spattered blood from the card and his knife on the dead man's coveralls. Silently, he left the ships hold.

As he made his escape down the ramp of the transport, out across the landing pad and towards the main building a small dark ship could just be seen overhead, trailing smoke. Its matt black hull and wedge shaped design resembled one of his own Krenaran ships, it seemed to be heading for the centre of Prague. However, its main weapon and torpedo launchers were completely different, deep indents in the sides of its hull gave off a bright electric blue light.

Lathiel recognised the ship as the Liberty, they must know of the plan, he thought, muttering a Krenaran curse; his job had just gotten that little bit more difficult.

12. A final reckoning.

Lathiel made his way calmly, yet quickly through the ten storey terminal building down the main elevator and out onto the busy roads outside.

He noticed a line of elaborately painted vehicles across the road. They all had signs above them with just one word, taxi, he wasn't sure what that meant, yet he needed to secure some form of transport so headed towards them anyway.

The driver looked at him quizzically, as the assassin was dressed in the inventory man's dirty coveralls, "do you have a destination."

"The institute of quantum mechanics," Lathiel replied with a smile, trying to act as naturally as he could.

"That's only a few minutes drive from here, hop in," the driver said.

Lathiel did so, and soon the unknowing driver was shepherding the assassin to his target.

The tall buildings of Prague whipped past like a blur as the battered form of the Liberty descended gradually towards its landing spot in the heart of Stromoika park.

"Deploy landing legs," Michael asked.

"Landing legs down," Eldathar replied.

Michael had hoped against hope that the landing legs were operational, otherwise the ship would slam front first straight into the park. Thank god for small mercies, he thought as the Liberty gently came in to land.

They could now see the wide open park, and the huge security cordon which had been hurriedly placed around it. The roads surrounding around the park had been blocked off and traffic had been steadily piling up, already the whole city looked largely gridlocked. The park itself was quickly cleared of any pedestrians, however a large crowd had gathered outside its confines to catch a glimpse of the landing of the most famous, or some would say infamous ship in the E.D.F.

The Liberty slowed almost to a standstill, then gently lowered itself onto its landing legs. It was a tight squeeze, the ship very nearly took up the entire length of the park. With a hiss of vented gas, the ship settled onto its legs and slowly began to power down.

"Eldathar, Dalvosh, Vargev, Kinraid, you're with me, we don't have much time."

Logameier came onto the bridge at the same time, "you might need these." He handed three Solarian scanners, one each to Michael, Vargev, and Kinraid. "They have been re-configured to be readable by humans."

"Logameier, you are in command until we get back," Michael said.

Lieutenant Johnson Logameier nodded his understanding, "good luck."

Vargev touched his wrist comm. "Commandoes, green light has been given, form up with us outside the Liberty."

The squad of E.D.F commandoes the Liberty had been carrying on its journey were ready. Vargev had briefed them earlier; they were nervous, this was not exactly the kind of mission commandoes were trained for. Nevertheless, Nikolai needed their raw skill and instinct for this most dangerous of foes.

The taxi had managed to make it to the rear of the institute, the driver turned in his seat to face him. "That's as close as I can get you, they have set up some sort of road block up ahead."

As the driver turned back to check his meter, Lathiel quickly took out one of his knives and rammed it straight through the drivers seat, impaling the taxi driver in the process. He slumped forward onto the steering wheel.

"That will be fine," Lathiel said as he quickly wiped the blood off the knife and hid it back within his coveralls, before exiting the taxi, and walking along the periphery of the institute, trying to fathom some way inside.

An E.D.F soldier was just coming into view around the side of the building on his security patrol, one hand on his pulse rifle and casting an eye over the nearby streets and tall buildings with their ancient teal coloured domes and tall ornate spires.

Lathiel made sure he attracted the guards attention, doing his utmost to make out that he was lost.

The guard approached him, "this area has been sealed off, you shouldn't be here."

Lathiel had checked for witnesses on the guards approach, there were none.

"Are you lost?" the guard asked.

"Yes I appear to be, I'm looking for a freight terminal, I'm due to pick up a delivery very soon, and I don't suppose you could point the way?"

The guard hesitated, thinking for a moment, "There is the...."

With a flash, Lathiel whipped out a knife and plunged it deep into the soldier's throat.

The man toppled backwards, gurgling, gasping and clutching at his ruin of a throat, blood spurted out from the wound, splattering to the pavement below.

Lathiel relieved the doomed soldier of his weapon, and opened fire at point blank range, ending the man's misery before dragging the body into a shadowed recess. Once he had dumped the body behind some bins he activated his crodes gland, once again acute pain ravaged his body, hopefully for the last time, he thought, as he gradually took on the form of the now deceased soldier.

Looking around this recessed area, he spied what appeared to be a fire exit. Using one of his knives, he managed, with a little effort, to push back the latch and open the door. Quietly he entered the institute, gently closing the door behind him.

Michael, Dalvosh, Vargev, Kinraid, Eldathar and the ten commandoes accompanying them, exited the Liberty and sprinted across the park towards the gigantic glass fronted building that was the institute of quantum mechanics, time was running out, they had to get to the assassin before he got to the president.

They each pulled out their new scanners as they approached, donated by some of the Solarian crewmembers onboard the Liberty. They were especially grateful, as it would be down to these things to help catch that killing machine.

Half a dozen E.D.F troops were stationed on guard at the main entrance as they approached.

"Halt!" Shouted a young stern sergeant, as the group raced towards him, the guards un-slung and readied their weapons.

"This is a secure area," he said as he looked upon the towering onrushing form of Dalvosh with hate-filled eyes.

"Look, the presidents life is in danger, we need to get in there, it's an emergency!" Michael shouted back.

"This is a secure area!" The sergeant repeated, louder this time.

Vargev came forward, together with his accompanying squad of commandoes. "Oh for gods sake, just let me through! You know who I am."

The young sergeant, full of bravado and machismo as he was, would not dare take on an E.D.F commando, as he knew full well their reputation. "Okay let them through," he said rather embarrassingly.

Vargev and the rest of the group simply elbowed their way past the guards, as he did so Vargev whispered vehemently to the sergeant. "If that president dies because you have held us up, I promise that no penal facility, no injury will come close to what I will do to you."

"err, yes sir," the sergeant said, his machismo evaporated.

The rest of the group all passed their new scanners over the guards, "they're all human," Eldathar said.

"Where is the president now?" Michael asked.

"In the main viewing area about to give his speech," the sergeant replied.

Michael turned to Kinraid, "You and Dalvosh inform the president, and watch out, this Lathiel is dangerous, he could be anyone."

"You sure that's wise?" Kinraid asked, "Dalvosh here isn't exactly te' most liked person on the planet right now."

Dalvosh nodded his agreement with Kinraid.

Michael knew the risk, however he also knew that, a Krenaran on earth, helping to save the life of the president himself might go someway to alleviate the intense mistrust and hatred humanity had of the Krenarans. "Yes I'm sure; go," he replied.

As they entered the main lobby of the building, Vargev turned to his accompanying squad of commandoes. "Okay I want you to split up; groups of two, I want a floor by floor search.

The commandoes all nodded their understanding, and began to fan out throughout the building, their heavy armschlagers ready, looking for the slightest hint of suspicious activity.

Vargev readied his own armschlager and Michael charged his pulse rifle. Eldathar took the lead as the three of them crossed the lobby and entered a narrow corridor. Along its length various types of laboratories split off from the corridor itself, a small party of scientists passed by the group.

"All human," Eldathar said as he scanned them. They continued on their search.

Lathiel made his way up a long steep flight of stairs, coming across a gantry above what appeared to be a series of gigantic magnets for an experiment of some kind.

A soldier on patrol casually walked towards him. "Hi" The man said as he calmly walked past the disguised killer.

"hi there," Lathiel replied as he continued walking across the gantry, this opened out into another corridor, as the assassin continued down it he came to a door that opened into a wide, yet small foyer.

Kinraid and Dalvosh had managed to make their way into the heavily crowded main viewing hall, they could see a large stage with a stand already prepared for the president.

The crowd gradually turned to look upon the towering form of the Krenaran that had come amongst them, and already the anger building in the room to this icon of hate was palpable. Dalvosh however ignored the insults and abuse hurled at him.

"There must be nearly five hundred people in here," Kinraid said.

"The perfect place for someone like Lathiel to hide," Dalvosh replied looking down at the Liberty first officer.

Cameras and equipment lined the periphery of the room, reporters spoke into them, no doubt capturing the big occasion for the various news services, some of the cameras swung in the direction of the giant Krenaran, standing head and shoulders above even the tallest people in the crowd. He stuck out like a sore thumb.

The two of them continued to force their way through the now hate filled crowd, the occasional bottle and other pieces of detritus was flung in the Krenarans general direction.

"I am not here to harm you, I am here to help!" Dalvosh shouted to the throng.

Shouts of, "tell it to the poor bastards you killed!" came flying back at him.

Eldathar, Michael and Vargev continued their search through the facility.

"Wait a second," Eldathar stopped looking at his scanner. "I'm picking up a Krenaran lifesign."

Vargev and Michael checked theirs too, "So are we, a Krenaran bio-sign seventy metres ahead and heading this way."

"You sure we are not picking up Dalvosh?" Vargev asked.

"No, this bio-sign is above us, Dalvosh is on the floor below."

"That's our man!" Michael shouted as the three of them sprinted towards the nearest flight of stairs.

Lathiel made his way through the foyer, and into a small, dark viewing room. There was a long floor to ceiling glass façade which ran the length of the room and offered a perfect view into the assembled crowd of the main viewing hall far below.

He un-slung his weapon and prepared the sight. The stage was empty right now, soon his target would take to the stage and when he did, the president of E.O.C.A would be no more. The Krenaran empire would have finally won this war, he would go back to his people a hero.

He saw that the crowd were jeering another Krenaran present; strange, he thought. Why should he be there? It mattered not; nothing would come between him and his mission, not even this other Krenaran. He put the thoughts to the back of his mind and peered through the rifle scope.

E.O.C.A President James Rushfeldt gracefully took to the stage dressed in an immaculately tailored suit and flanked by two bodyguards, waving to the crowd assembled in front of him.

"This is a momentous day, barely a week ago humanity and the Krenaran race were still locked in a bitter war, and now a Krenaran stands on Earth as a symbol of peace; please, won't you join me?"

The lights and cameras turned towards the powerful lumbering form of Dalvosh as he gradually made his way through the throng, every single man and woman who looked upon his towering reptilian form half covered in shining metallic Krenaran battle armour, looked upon it with hate-filled eyes.

Gradually Dalvosh took to the stage next to the president, who quickly switched off the microphones arrayed in front of him.

"I've just done you a huge favour, your not here to kill me, you would have done that already. So what the hell are you doing here?" Rushfeldt looked up at the Krenaran.

"We're here to save you," Dalvosh growled back. "There is a rogue Krenaran agent loose in the building, and you are his target."

Rushfeldt froze, "where?"

"We don't know yet, the building is being searched right now."

Michael, Eldathar, and Vargev sprinted up a flight of stairs breathing heavily as they did so, Eldathar's gangly Solarian legs carried him much faster than the others.

"Twenty meters," Michael puffed, "just beyond that corridor."

They sprinted for all they were worth, preying they weren't too late, accidentally knocking over a cleaning woman in their haste.

Together they burst through the door of the dimly lit viewing room, and were confronted with the sight of an E.D.F soldier pointing a pulse rifle to the viewing glass.

Eldathar held up his scanner first, "that's him!"

Michael was fastest, sprinting across the room he lunged in a desperate attempted to knock the assassin off balance before he got a shot away, just as he was about to press the trigger. Michael slammed into Lathiel as the shot fired, shattering the glass, it was just enough for the shot to miss the president. Instead however, it slammed into the chest of Dalvosh who was thrown backwards by the force of the impact.

The crowd panicked and began to rush headlong for the exits, people were knocked aside, several were being crushed in the press of people desperate to escape.

The momentum of Michael's charge proved too much and Lathiel used his own speed and weight against him, as he pushed him flying through another glass pane; shattering it too as Michael's body sailed through it.

Shards of smashed glass rained down on the already panicked crowd below, as the sheer force of people charging towards him flattened Kinraid. Dalvosh lay face up on the stage, the two bodyguards ignored the fallen Krenaran, instead rapidly ushering the president out of the room through an emergency exit behind them.

Michael desperately clung to a length of steel pipe-work directly below the overhanging viewing room, thankfully the pipe was cool; there he dangled forty feet in the air, his legs flailing wildly as his weapon clattered onto the marble floor some forty feet below. The pain in his arm was excrutiating, he had wrenched his shoulder badly grabbing onto the pipe.

Vargev and Eldathar confronted Lathiel. Eldathar attempted to tackle the assassin, Lathiel was much faster than the gangly Solarian and without a word flung one of his knives at him. Eldathar screamed out in pain as the blade embedded itself in his arm, sending out a gout of blue-ish blood, the force of the blade pinned the Solarian pilot to the wall.

Lathiel, angered at having his mission interrupted, menacingly drew his second blade.

Vargev dropped his Armschlager and drew his own combat knife. The assassin and the Russian silently and menacingly circled each other, sizing one another up.

Lathiel was the first to attack, lashing out with his blade the knife was a blur as it flicked out. Vargev barely had time to dodge the slash as Lathiel pounced again. This time Vargev was able to parry the blow, both their blades locked together. Rapidly bringing up his knee, the Krenaran impostor rammed it into the Russians stomach; he staggered backwards a few steps as pain coursed through his already fragile ribs.

The assassin swiped at him again, the blade sliced deep into the flesh of Vargev's upper right arm. The Russian screamed in pain, clutching at his wound.

"Don't make me laugh old man," Lathiel spat as he viciously spin-kicked Vargev in the chest, sending him sprawling across the hard floor; his knife clattered across the ground.

For a moment fear began to rise in Vargev, this man was his equal, and may yet beat him. He banished the thought and got to his feet, still clutching his wounded arm.

"Huh, still some fight left in you….okay then," Lathiel said with a cruel sneer, as he tossed the commando back his knife, daring him to fight on.

Vargev picked the knife back up just as the assassin lunged at him again; barely managing to parry the blow, he was knocked backwards once again.

Lathiel let out a sarcastic laugh.

"I'm still standing," Vargev shot back.

"Not for much longer." He came at the Russian again, stabbing and slashing, this time Vargev was able to counter the blows, parried the blade and unleashed a vicious head-butt of his own. The imposter cried in pain, stumbled backwards as blood coursed down his ruined nose. As the assassin stumbled backward momentarily dazed, Vargev seized his chance plunging his knife deep into Lathiel's stomach.

The assassin gasped; spluttering out a gobbet of blood across Vargev's face just as the Russian charged, propelling the assassin straight through the broken glass panels, and sending the disguised Krenaran hurtling to the now almost completely empty marble floor far below, slamming into it with a sickeningly wet crunch.

The wounded Vargev stood at the edge of the platform, gripping his blood-soaked right arm and looked down solemnly at the broken form of Lathiel his Russian eyes gave just a hint of respect for a worthy opponent, after all the assassin was easily capable of killing him instead. Then he noticed Michael precariously dangling from the steel pipe, and gradually hauled him back up inside the viewing room.

"It's over comrade, it's finally over."

The pain seared through the Russians arm once again, his torn camouflaged fatigues stained with blood. Together they helped Eldathar free himself from Lathiels knife blade stuck through his arm, the Solarian howled in pain as they freed the blade, a welter of azure blue blood coursed down the Solarian's arm, he was weak but managed to get back to his feet.

In the main viewing hall below, Dalvosh and Kinraid gradually recovered, and got back to their feet also, the commander looked rather battered, and sporting several bruises after being practically crushed from the panicking crowd.

"You're alive, I thought that shot had killed you," he said to the hulking Krenaran.

"My battle armour dissipated the energy, just the impact staggered me," the Krenaran replied, rubbing his sore reptilian head.

The rest of the commandoes had converged on Vargev's position, and helped the wounded forms of their commander and Eldathar. They were gradually helped back out of the building where a waiting medical team rushed to tend to their wounds.

President Rushfeldt approached them; all that had remained of the crowds that had been there were Michael's team, the commandoes and a smattering of E.D.F troops.

"I've just heard what happened inside there, my people didn't think it would be a good idea to return, but I had to. I want to thank you all from the bottom of my heart; your heroics saved my life."

"Just doing our job Mr. President," Michael replied.

Rushfeldt then turned to Dalvosh, "barely a week ago we were implacable enemies locked in a bitter conflict, and killing each other by the thousand. And now you risked your life to protect a people who absolutely hate you and everything about your race, why?"

"Because it was the right thing to do, the war was over, and Lathiel was rogue, his actions threatened to destabilise the entire peace process."

Rushfeldt considered this for a moment, genuinely moved by the actions of these brave few, "maybe one day there could be a lasting peace between our peoples."

"Krenarans and Terrans are two completely different societies, with totally different cultures, however in time their may yet be a true peace, however there is a lot of pain and hate on both our sides."

13. The rebuilding.

A week after the events in Prague, Colonel Nikolai Vargev emerged through a set of automatic hospital doors, his arm still heavily bandaged. Fumbling around inside his brightly coloured cotton civilian shirt pocket, he fished out one of his trademark cigars.

Taking out his lighter, he lit the end of it and began slowly puffing on it. Crossing the busy street from the hospital he made his way over to a small apartment block nearby, which was renting for him, while he recovered from his injuries.

Climbing the concrete stairwell up to the fourth floor, and making his way down a dank, dimly lit corridor, he made his way to his temporary apartment. Closing the door behind him gently, and the big Russian poured himself a small glass of vodka, stroked his dark moustache, and sat at the communications terminal. Keying in a few commands with his one good hand he contacted Michael who he knew was overseeing the ongoing repair work to the Liberty at alpha base.

His face flashed up on the screen, "Hello Nikolai."

Vargev nodded, "Hello captain, how are the repairs going, I guess they are not going to scrap her after all then."

Michael smiled, "not if I have anything to say about it, it will be another month before she is operational again. I've given the crew shore leave while the repairs are completed. There is even talk about a few more upgrades."

"You do realise, they will most likely make you an admiral for this." Vargev said taking a gentle sip from his glass.

"They already offered; I turned it down. Told them I was perfectly happy commanding the Liberty, besides there is plenty of life left in the old bird yet anyway."

Vargev smiled, "Guess what, I've got another medal ceremony coming my way. This time the star cross for bravery, I'm getting quite a tally," he joked.

"You just like all the attention, what's next for the commandoes?"

"Mainly peacetime operations, some peacekeeping duties while the outer colonies start to re-build, mine clearing, that sort of thing. The E.D.F are concerned about piracy and looters while the re-building process begins."

"Uh huh, well the next outing for the Liberty once she's back up and running is escorting a bunch of transports returning former P.O.W's back to their homes, and then anti-pirate duties ourselves. E.D.F command expects pirate cartels to increase while the rebuilding is under way also."

"Well my friend, it has been good working with you again, perhaps our paths will cross in the future......who knows?"

"Who knows indeed, goodbye old friend."

With that, Nikolai ended the communication, gently sat back in his leather armchair, and turned on the viewer.

"I am Annika Raumov, and this is the outer colony news service, the headlines tonight. Two weeks after the end of the Krenaran war, one of the bloodiest periods in recent history. The first refugees are beginning to make their way back to the devastated outer colonies that were once their homes, tentative re-building work has already begun however analysts predict that a full recovery could well take up to a decade."

Nikolai Vargev turned off the viewer, took a sip of vodka and sat back in his chair, humanity will recover, we will survive and we will go on. The thought gave him a warm feeling.

The End.

About the author.

Born in Cheshire, England in 1981, to a traditional family, Ian's mother is a housewife and his father worked in industry and is a retired Heavy Goods Vehicle driver.

Ian developed an affinity for Science Fiction and fantasy at a very early age, and was reading various fantasy and SF novels from the age of 8. The phenomenon that was Star trek, Star wars, and various Sci-fi shows came to his attention during his early years in high school, and it was here where Ian's creative writing really began to take root.

His english teachers would from time to time give him the occasional creative writing exercise to complete, and he always loved doing these, and excelled at them. His teachers noted that one of his main strengths was in fact creative writing, possessing of a boundless imagination which shows through in his writing.

As Ian grew older and the world of work beckoned, his writing began to wane, although the ideas were still there bubbling under the surface. It was during this time when he first began to come up with the idea for E.D.F chronicles, which would linger in the back of his mind for almost a decade.

Finally, in 2007, after much upheaval in his personal life, he took up the pen and began writing seriously, completing the first draft of the Krenaran massacre in just three months while spending some time out in Bulgaria with family; although it took almost 2 years for it to become a fully written manuscript.

Now completed the sequel to his debut novel E.D.F resurgent, Ian is working on the third book in the series Eye of the Dracos, due for release in 2012.

Website http://www.wix.com/ian_smethurst/frontpage
Blog http://edfchronicles.wordpress.com/

www.ingramcontent.com/pod-product-compliance
Lightning Source LLC
Chambersburg PA
CBHW021116130626
46554CB00002B/718